***A thrilling new duology from Harlequin Presents
and Harlequin Medical Romance!***

Royally Tempted

…at the first incendiary glance!

Castilona royals are used to unimaginable wealth and privilege, so when one falls ill, only the best treatment the island kingdom's coffers can buy will do. But a visit to Clínica San Carlos may change the course of the monarchy's future…

When King Octavio spent one red-hot night in the comforting arms of hospital cleaner Phoebe, he never anticipated her falling pregnant—with twins. The only reasonable royal solution? Demanding her hand in marriage!

Twins for His Majesty by Clare Connelly

Available now from Harlequin Presents!

Princess Xiomara will only allow the world's top fetal surgeon to treat her cousin's wife and the kingdom's unborn heirs. Even if Dr. Edmund ignites her deepest desires…

Forbidden Fling with the Princess by Amy Andrews

When a hurricane hits, head of hospital security— Xiomara's illegitimate half brother—Xavier and clinical director Lola are stuck at Clínica San Carlos overnight. With a storm of passion raging between them!

One Night to Royal Baby by JC Harroway

Both available now from Harlequin Medical Romance!

Dear Reader,

It's not often in medical romances one gets to write a princess let alone inventing an Island kingdom *and* a fictional royal family, so I was super excited to be part of this cross series project with Clare Connelly and JC Harroway.

One of the things I like most about writing medicals is the emotional connection that is forged when the hero and heroine are plunged into high stakes medical situations. Edmund and Xiomara epitomize such a situation, having to ignore their attraction as they work together to save the royal twin babies. When that's done though? When they get to be just Ed and Xio? That's when the sparks really start to fly.

But how can a world famous obstetric surgeon and a royal princess, who inhabit very different worlds with competing demands on their time, ever truly hope to forge a life together when they can barely have a few secret days away without becoming a paparazzi sensation?

I hope you enjoy the stakes and the sizzle between the doctor and the princess from that first dramatic meeting on a Seychelles beach to their eventual, hard-earned HEA.

Big love,

Amy

FORBIDDEN FLING WITH THE PRINCESS

AMY ANDREWS

MEDICAL ROMANCE

If you purchased this book without a cover you should be aware that this book is stolen property. It was reported as "unsold and destroyed" to the publisher, and neither the author nor the publisher has received any payment for this "stripped book."

ISBN-13: 978-1-335-99323-6

Forbidden Fling with the Princess

Copyright © 2025 by Amy Andrews

All rights reserved. No part of this book may be used or reproduced in any manner whatsoever without written permission.

Without limiting the author's and publisher's exclusive rights, any unauthorized use of this publication to train generative artificial intelligence (AI) technologies is expressly prohibited.

This is a work of fiction. Names, characters, places and incidents are either the product of the author's imagination or are used fictitiously. Any resemblance to actual persons, living or dead, businesses, companies, events or locales is entirely coincidental.

For questions and comments about the quality of this book, please contact us at CustomerService@Harlequin.com.

TM and ® are trademarks of Harlequin Enterprises ULC.

 Harlequin Enterprises ULC
22 Adelaide St. West, 41st Floor
Toronto, Ontario M5H 4E3, Canada
www.Harlequin.com

HarperCollins Publishers
Macken House, 39/40 Mayor Street Upper,
Dublin 1, D01 C9W8, Ireland
www.HarperCollins.com

Printed in U.S.A.

Amy Andrews is a multi-award-winning, *USA TODAY* bestselling Australian author who has written over fifty contemporary romances in both the traditional and digital markets. She loves good books, fab food, great wine and frequent travel—preferably all four together. To keep up with her latest releases, news, competitions and giveaways, sign up for her newsletter—amyandrews.com.au.

Books by Amy Andrews

Harlequin Medical Romance

How to Mend a Broken Heart
Evie's Bombshell
One Night She Would Never Forget
How to Resist Temptation
The Tortured Hero
It Happened One Night Shift
Swept Away by the Seductive Stranger
A Christmas Miracle
Tempted by Mr. Off-Limits
Nurse's Outback Temptation
Harper and the Single Dad

Visit the Author Profile page
at Harlequin.com for more titles.

To Clare and Jo. It's been an absolute blast
spending time in a fictious Mediterranean kingdom
with you both. Let's do it for real, sometime!

**Praise for
Amy Andrews**

"Packed with humor, heart and pathos, *Swept Away
by the Seductive Stranger* is a stirring tale of second
chances, redemption and hope with a wonderfully
feisty and intelligent heroine you will adore and a
gorgeous hero whom you will love."

—*Goodreads*

CHAPTER ONE

FOR THE FIRST time in five years, Edmund Butler had nowhere to go and nothing to do. No pager to rule his life. And he was making the most of it on a Seychelles beach where the sun was hot and the beers were cold. There was peace. Serenity. Sand so white it hurt his eyes. Water so clear it could have come from an ancient Scottish burn.

He needed this. He *really* needed this.

As he reached for his second of the four beer bottles in the bucket, he became aware of the distant thump of rotor blades but he paid them no heed. Joy flights ran regularly across the various islands of the archipelago.

Cracking the top, Ed took three long swallows then pulled the lever on his deckchair until he was fully reclined. The chair had been conveniently placed on the sand beneath the fronds of a gently swaying palm on a deserted stretch of beach, although given the tiny exclusive island only ever hosted two dozen people, everywhere was pretty much deserted.

Shutting his eyes behind his Polaroid sunglasses, he let out a deep, contented exhale and tuned into the gentle swish of the tide as it lapped

8   FORBIDDEN FLING WITH THE PRINCESS

at the beach. The steady *thump, thump, thump* got louder however, obliterating the mellow ebb and flow of the ocean and Ed briefly considered stripping off his board shorts and giving the occupants a real show. He didn't, but it made him smile as he waited lazily for the chopper to *buzz* off.

Unfortunately, it did not.

It got so loud he actually raised his head to discover it was coming in to land on the spit of sand at the far end of the beach. Intrigued, he levered himself upright and idly watched as the surface of the water rippled violently beneath the downwash. There was a glossiness to the chopper that reeked of wealth with its sleek indigo fuselage, dark tinted windows and no identifying logos. It certainly wasn't like any of the commercial ones he'd seen doing scenic flights the past few days.

Maybe it was a private hire? A celebrity?

Moments later, the skids kissed terra firma, kicking up a cloud of white sand. The engine cut immediately, reducing the powdery veil and the level of noise, but the whine of the rotors as they slowed still reached him on the breeze.

With the blades not yet come to a standstill, the side door suddenly opened. Out stepped a brawny guy in dark fatigues. He had a military-style haircut, aviator sunglasses, black boots and an equally black gun holstered at his hip.

Private security? Yep, probably a celebrity.

The guy turned and offered his hand to a second occupant who took it as *she* exited barefoot, in a flurry of honey-brown curls and liquid silver fabric whipped around from the rotor draught. Ed caught a glimpse of bare bronzed arms as the woman lifted one hand to her hair and the other to her skirt that was threatening to go full Marilyn as she was ushered out from under the blades. The fluttery fabric, which seemed as though it would be more at home on a Parisian catwalk than on a beach, was perilously close to taking off.

Finally, as the couple moved far enough from the chopper, the mystery woman shook her head, her hair bouncing back into place to reveal her face. She was very *movie star* in a pair of large, impossibly cool sunglasses, her lips popping in a vibrant shade of red, her mouth as full and lush as the curves beneath the silvery silk that dazzled like tin foil in the sunshine.

The high halter neckline of her dress exposed her shoulders and clung to her full breasts. Belted loosely at the waist, the generous fabric in the skirt moved like liquid metal in the light tropical breeze, outlining the generous proportions of her hips and thighs and fluttering behind her like the tail of a kite.

Statuesque with a coppery complexion, everything about her screamed *celebrity*. Not that she was familiar to Ed, but that didn't mean much given he wasn't one for gossip magazines or tabloid dross. She certainly moved in that way that

10   FORBIDDEN FLING WITH THE PRINCESS

people with means and money always moved, like recognition was not only expected but foregone.

Ed took another sip of his beer as she was escorted, he assumed, to the resort reception, which meant she'd have to pass by his chair. With her armed protection by her side, it was quite the show but, whoever she was, she'd probably come here to *not* be ogled by strangers. The resort was the ultimate in discreet relaxation and he wasn't about to spoil that vibe so he lowered the back of the chair again, stretched his legs out and shut his eyes.

The last thing he expected was for her to approach him.

'Ah-*hem*.'

Ed's eyes flicked open in surprise to find the woman and her security guard looking down on him. Well, *she* was looking down at him, the guy in black was standing at a discreet distance scanning the nearby tree line and ocean as if he was expecting an imminent attack. Their approach had been ninja-like.

The sand, he supposed.

She was even more gorgeous up close, her smooth caramel complexion unblemished, her red lips screaming *look at me*, curves somehow more tempting stationary than when they'd been moving.

Or maybe that was just because they were in easier reach.

'I'm sorry to interrupt your relaxation,' she apologised, a slight accent to her polished English, 'but you are Edmund Butler, yes? Dr Edmund Butler?'

Ed was pleased that his sunglasses hid his surprise. There were parts of this world where he was very well known. Considered a rock star, even, his services in high demand. But not here on this island in the middle of the Indian Ocean where he was just Ed from London.

'Yes,' he confirmed warily as he reached for the handle of his deckchair and levered himself upright, placing his half consumed beer bottle in the bucket of ice.

The action caused her to straighten and take a step back. 'Perfect.' She nodded, relieved, and held out her hand. 'My name is Princess Xiomara de la Rosa of Castilona and I need your help.'

Ed's surprise morphed to suspicion. Ignoring her hand, he looked to the left and right, wondering where the cameras might be, because surely, he was being pranked right now? He was involved in a longstanding game of *gotcha* with a bunch of his old med school buddies. It had been growing more elaborate over the years as their pay cheques had expanded but this was next level.

A *princess* of some place he'd never heard of, and therefore probably didn't exist, had landed in a helicopter asking for *his help*? Like Princess goddamn Leia?

'Okay, funny.' He nodded and let out a fake *ha-ha* laugh. 'Did Julian send you?' Dr Julian Bosworth was a grown-ass endocrinologist at the cutting edge of pancreatic research but still acted like he was on freshers' week at Cambridge.

He was also a massive *Star Wars* fan.

She gave a somewhat pained smile as her hand dropped. 'I'm sorry, I don't know any Julian and I understand this is unusual—'

'It's Thacks, isn't it?' Ed interrupted, pulling off his glasses, staring at the tree line behind him now with even more scrutiny than the guy in fatigues. 'You can come out Thacker, joke's over.'

Harry Thacker had perhaps been the smartest of the lot of them, choosing to go into dermatology, where there was no on-call and no weekends and no shortage of people willing to pay boatloads of money to keep their skin looking young. And he had a garage full of fancy motor vehicles to prove it. He'd been hatching something ever since Ed had set up that fake email about his brand-new high-end imported sports car being lost overboard somewhere in the English Channel.

'I can assure you, Dr Butler, this is no joke and I am who I say I am.'

She turned to her bodyguard and spoke to him in what sounded like Spanish. He stepped forward, delving into the left pocket of his shirt, extracting what looked like a passport, and handed it to her before returning to his previous position. She held it out to Ed who, bemused, accepted it, noting immediately the bold gold letters pronouncing it to be a *Diplomatic Passport*.

Okay, it looked *real*, but in this day and age this kind of thing could be easily faked to be realistic enough for someone who wasn't trained in forgery detection. Xiomara Maria Fernanda de la Rosa— *sheesh*, what a mouthful. His gaze was drawn to the photograph, which was her but also wasn't. Her curls were pulled ruthlessly back into a sleek topknot with not one hair out of place, the neckline of her shirt hugged her throat and her lipstick was a demure shade of pink.

And then there was her hundred-yard stare peeping out from those green eyes that seemed very poised and *regal* and maybe even a little sad.

'Nice try,' he said, handing it back. 'But I set up an entire fake website and account for a car company in two hours. I'm not that gullible.'

Her red mouth tightening, she too removed her sunglasses to reveal barely concealed impatience glowing in the golden flecks of her green eyes. 'Why don't you Google me?' she suggested with an imperial air that was painstakingly polite, leaving Ed in little doubt that even suggesting it was beneath her. She folded her arms. 'I'll wait.'

Ed blinked. Whoever this woman was, she was a very good actress. Thacks had done well.

Realising this wasn't going to be over until he did so, Ed grabbed his phone that was sitting on the tray next to his bucket of beer and Googled

14   FORBIDDEN FLING WITH THE PRINCESS

the Princess. The first image in the search was an official portrait of the royal house of de la Rosa with the woman standing in front of him staring, poised and elegant—a *tiara* on her head—at the camera. The caption beneath informed him it was from earlier in the year at the coronation of King Octavio of Castilona, which was apparently a small island kingdom off the coast of Spain.

There were pages and pages of images. Some formal—perfect royal smile outlined in varying shades of pink as she performed some duty or other. Some clearly taken by paparazzi—gritty, grainy, distant. *Waaay* less formal, including one in an electric-blue one-piece, standing ankle-deep in an ocean somewhere, her hair a mass of careless waves springing around her head.

All of them proved that she was indeed who she said she was.

Ed glanced up from his phone to find her passively waiting his response. 'Okay.' He tossed his phone on the recliner. 'You're a princess. Apologies.'

Xiomara waved her hand dismissively in a way he assumed she waved to crowds from her goldencrusted horse-drawn coach. 'It's fine. Shall we start again? My name is Xiomara de la Rosa. I'm very pleased to make your acquaintance, Dr Butler.'

She presented her hand again, not in a *let's shake* way but in a very *papal* here-is-my-ring way. Ed sure as hell hoped she didn't expect him to kiss it. He wasn't opposed to kissing this stunning woman, but her hand would not be the first choice of where to put his lips.

Swinging his legs around, he pushed into a standing position, which saw the guy behind her tense, his hand automatically hovering over his holstered weapon. Ignoring him as much as it was possible to ignore a clearly ex-military guy *and a princess* on a beach in the Seychelles, he encased her hand in his, giving it a brisk shake before withdrawing. The guard relaxed his stance and went back to surveilling the surroundings.

'I'm sorry, have we met before?'

Ed had met a lot of people throughout his career, both in the UK and around the world. He'd even met royalty. But he was pretty sure he'd have remembered a European princess and, in particular, *her.* But why else would she come looking for *him*?

And, more importantly, how in the hell had she known *where* he was?

'No.' She shook her head. 'We are unacquainted. But I have a problem and you are the solution. My cousin, the King…his wife is pregnant with twins and the latest scan shows major issues and I would like you to accompany me to Castilona to advise and treat.'

If Ed hadn't already established Xiomara was the real deal, he'd definitely be thinking he was being pranked right now. His brain—usually able

16   FORBIDDEN FLING WITH THE PRINCESS

to juggle myriad complex tasks including in utero foetal surgery—was blanking out. There were so many questions crowding around up there, he plucked the first one he could latch on to.

'How did you know I was here?'

Maybe not the most important question of the many but he was on *holiday*. For two blissful weeks. His first one in five years. Then he was going to Africa as part of an NGO to train doctors in foetal medicine. And the only people who knew his current location were his parents, his close friends, his PA and a few people within the NGO.

She lifted a bare shoulder in a dismissive shrug. 'My cousin is a *king*. We have our ways.'

Ed's gaze flicked to the hired muscle, struck by how absurd it all seemed. He couldn't help but feel as if he'd landed in the middle of a James Bond film, what with a princess landing in a helicopter and a foreign nation knowing his exact whereabouts.

But the absurdity quickly morphed to irritability and then to affront.

This *wasn't* a movie. This was his life. His *real* life. And he was a private citizen. So whatever was going on with the King's twins and no matter how much he might have very much enjoyed her company in another set of circumstances, Princess Xiomara and her *ways* could get back on that helicopter and fly home.

'I'm sorry but I deal in a very specialized area of foetal medicine.' It was his turn for strained politeness. As much as he wanted to tell her to kiss his ass, she *was* royalty and he *was* British. And even if his humble roots chafed at the concept of unelected hereditary rule there was no need to be rude. 'I could certainly recommend someone for your cousin and his wife.'

His attempt at being reductive to her royal pedigree was a tad petty but *he was on holiday.*

'Dr Edmund Butler,' she said, those golden specks in her eyes flashing again. 'Fellow of the Royal College of Obstetricians and Gynaecologists, head of the Intrauterine Surgical Alliance, chair of the World Symposium of Foetal Surgery, founder of the Foetal Surgical Research Institute, author of over seven-hundred peer reviewed journal articles that have been cited over fifty thousand times, the leading expert on endoscopic laser surgery for Twin-to-Twin Transfusion Syndrome.' She folded her arms. 'You are exactly who I need.'

Well, okay then. She'd done her research.

'I have all the details in a file in the helicopter but, briefly, Queen Phoebe is twenty-two weeks pregnant with twins. A routine ultrasound has just identified stage one TTTS.'

Despite the fact he was *on a beach, under a palm tree, in his board shorts, on his first holiday in five years,* Ed's brain clicked over. Stage one could just require close monitoring or could

18   FORBIDDEN FLING WITH THE PRINCESS

quickly evolve into a situation that required immediate action. The scan results would help but performing his own ultrasound would be the best way for him to get a feel for this particular scenario.

Wait. *No.* He was on holiday, *damn it.*

'Well, as you can see—' he gestured around '—I'm currently on holiday. But I can put you in touch with three other top foetal surgeons, all who are colleagues of mine in London and excellent at their jobs. I'm sure any one of them would be more than happy to advise and or treat as required.'

Ed's earlier Googling had informed him Xiomara was twenty-seven, but if he thought her relative youth would make her easily cowed, he was wrong. Her poised royal vibes were more than a match for his hard-earned leading expert persona. Although he supposed it was difficult to look like the leading expert in *anything* dressed in nothing but a pair of floral board shorts.

'But *you* are the best, yes?'

'Yes.' Ed saw little point in denying what was established fact.

'Then it is only you I want.'

Her chin jutted determinedly and Ed was left in no doubt Princess Xiomara was unused to being denied. Which was too bad for her because he was starting to get really ticked off. A state which had been exacerbated by the crazy lurch in his pulse at her *it is only you I want.* In a more…romantic setting he might have appreciated her direct lan-

AMY ANDREWS 19

guage, but right now he resented that his traitorous body was all *team curvy princess*.

'Unfortunately, I am currently unavailable. Something I could have just as easily conveyed over the phone, along with my recommendations. Given you know my whereabouts, I assume you also have my number.'

A slight smile flitted briefly across her red mouth in a silent kind of *touché*. 'I didn't want you to tell me no.'

'I'm telling you no, now.'

Another chin jut as she glanced disparagingly at the bucket of beers. 'You don't appear to be doing anything very much at the moment.'

'That *is* the point of a holiday.'

'Drinking beer at ten in the morning?'

Okay, he was done with this now. Given his almost perpetual on-call state, Ed rarely consumed alcohol so if he wanted to drink beer all day, every day whilst *on vacation*, he was going to do exactly that and not be shamed by a posh little miss who'd probably never worked a day in her life.

'Listen, lady—'

'Actually,' she interrupted, that red mouth of hers twitching almost imperceptibly, 'it's Your Royal Highness.'

Ed lifted an eyebrow. Yeah, he wasn't going to call her that. And yet, despite his irritation, he was impressed with her arrogance. Up until this point, he didn't think he'd ever met anyone more

20   FORBIDDEN FLING WITH THE PRINCESS

conceited than a specialty surgeon but she'd definitely blown that out of the water.

'*Xiomara*,' he conceded. She might have a royal pedigree but his medical pedigree was not to be sneezed at, nor was *he* easily intimidated. 'I'm afraid you've wasted your time here today.'

Clearly not deterred by his dismissal, she continued. 'We will, of course, ensure you are adequately compensated.'

Ed shot her a sardonic smile. 'I don't need your money. I have plenty of my own.'

Okay, he didn't have *princess* money, but he commanded a high-end salary, owned an apartment in Kensington, drove an expensive car and had made wise investments. Not bad for a kid who'd grown up being home schooled in whatever hotspot his humanitarian aid worker parents were in at the time.

'One hundred thousand pounds.'

Ed blinked. *What the...?* Was she joking right now? Her calm expression, the way she held his gaze without batting an eyelid, told him she was serious. He shook his head. 'No.'

Without skipping a beat, she increased the offer. 'Two hundred thousand pounds.'

Folding his arms, Ed stared her down. 'No.'

'Three hundred thousand pounds.'

'No.'

'Four hundred thousand pounds.'

'*Xiomara*.' He gave an exasperated shake of his

head, trying to decide whether to be annoyed or, frankly, a little turned on by a woman splashing around cash to get her own way. To get *him* to do her bidding.

'You want more?'

'You could offer me a million pounds and the answer would still be no. You invade my privacy, you shatter my peace and quiet, you disregard the fact I'm on holiday and then you arrogantly assume I can be bought? The answer is *no*.'

She raised one thick, perfectly coiffed eyebrow. 'So you will see the twins die because you're annoyed at my methods?'

'Just as well there are several other specialists who can help you.'

'Five hundred thousand.'

Ed laughed then. What else could he do? It was comically ridiculous. 'You cannot be serious right now?'

'Look at my face, Dr Butler.' Her features morphed from quietly determined to bullishly resolute. 'You think I do not take the lives of my cousin's unborn twins and future sovereigns of my country seriously?'

'Clearly, when there are very viable alternatives, you do not.'

'The King and Queen of Castilona deserve the best and that is what they will get. Seven hundred and fifty thousand pounds.'

He sighed. 'No.'

Pressing her lips flat, she regarded him for a long moment. Ed wasn't sure how she managed to look down her nose at him when he had her by a few inches, but somehow, she did.

'One million pounds donated to your Foetal Surgical Research Institute.'

Ed had opened his mouth to tell Xiomara no again but, after a stunned beat, clicked it shut. Well...*crap.* That kind of money bought a lot of research potential to an organisation who relied on charitable donations to do their valuable work.

Princess Xiomara de la Rosa of Castilona had found his Achilles heel.

CHAPTER TWO

XIOMARA TOOK IN the coral reefs fringing the island as it grew smaller and smaller below them, the rotor noise above almost non-existent thanks to the superb soundproofing inside the luxuriously appointed helicopter. The Indian Ocean sparkled like a jewel, the clear waters forming a demarcation between the warmer shallows and the sapphire layers of the deep.

Opposite her in a plush white leather seat sat Xavier Torres, wearing earphones with an angled mouthpiece to communicate with the cockpit. Castilonian by birth, his mother a cook in the royal kitchens, Xavier had spent time away in the military before a roadside explosion had affected his sight in one eye, precipitating his return. He'd been part of the royal family protection detail ever since and assigned to her for the last three years. Mostly he kept her shielded from the paparazzi but, as per royal protocols, he accompanied her wherever she was on business for the monarchy.

Beside her on a white leather bench seat sat a bare-chested, barefoot, board-short wearing world-renowned expert in fetoscopic photocoagulation surgery for Twin-to-Twin Transfusion Syndrome.

Mission accomplished.

Xiomara had been underestimated her entire life. As a female in a monarchy dominated by a male succession line, she had been raised to be a *princess*. Despite being well educated, articulate and capable, she'd been reduced to hostess duties—cutting pretty ribbons, making pretty speeches and looking pretty in official family photographs.

Her father, Mauricio, had ruled Castilona as Regent for almost a decade, stepping in for his young nephew, Octavio, who'd only been nine when his parents—King Miguel and Queen Eleanora—had died in a car accident. Mauricio, Miguel's twin and younger by two minutes, was a cruel and bitter man who had been a distant father with high standards and low morals.

He had only ever seen Xiomara as a chess piece to move around a board, expecting her to be seen and rarely heard. His to show off when it suited, and to neglect when it did not. If her mother had not intervened on several occasions, she would already be married to a man of his choosing and producing royal babies. Royal *boy* babies to secure the line *should something happen to Octavio* who, constitutionally, hadn't been able to rule until he turned twenty-eight.

Every time her father had said that, it had put an itch up her spine.

Thankfully, Octavio had come of age—unharmed—recently and finally ascended the throne. Xiomara had been thrilled for her cousin, not least because her father's power over him, the country *and herself* had been broken. But mostly because, like his father Miguel, Octavio was a good, smart, honourable man that Mauricio's poison had never managed to undermine.

Xiomara and Tavi, as she affectionately called him, had always been close and to see him sitting on the throne where he should rightfully have been a long time ago, were it not for archaic constitutional clauses, gave her such joy.

For him and Castilona.

Seeing him meet then fall in love with Phoebe and their excitement over her pregnancy had been an utter delight. So, when this devastating news about the babies had come to light, she'd been determined to fix it for them.

To prove her mettle. To prove, once and for all, she should never again be underestimated merely because she'd been born a girl.

Within two hours, she'd identified the exact doctor they needed for the royal babies and Tavi, who had been dealing with not only his own emotions and an anxious Phoebe but also ever-present matters of state, had entrusted *her* to go get him.

Finally being given something worthwhile to

do and with the full force of the de la Rosa name on her side, Xiomara had gone full steam ahead.

Of course, the man in question hadn't made it easy. Not finding him nor getting him to agree.

She couldn't remember the last person—her father excepted—who had not automatically acquiesced to her, so his *no* had been quite a revelation. But had also, rather strangely, intrigued her. She'd *liked* that he hadn't gone all obsequious when she'd introduced herself. That he hadn't known—*nor particularly cared*—who she was.

She'd *liked* that he hadn't felt cowed by her status and folded to her demands.

Edmund Butler had challenged her. Had pushed her. And Xiomara had been there for it. She'd felt truly alive in those moments they'd verbally sparred. And the way he'd said *yes* when she'd asked him if he was the best. No demurring, no false modesty, no self-deprecating dismissal of his prowess. Just *yes*. All deep and sure. Some might even have said conceited.

Arrogant. Egotistical.

But she'd read all about him and Edmund Butler's ego was writing cheques his body could definitely cash. In *every* sense of the word. Barely dressed on a Seychelles beach he'd been a sight to behold. His broad shoulders and magnificent chest—sporting a ladder of puckered abs and a smattering of hair in all the right places—had taken up every inch of her peripheral vision, sparking a very inconvenient frisson of awareness.

A frisson that was still vibrating through her body.

Perhaps that had been why it had taken her so long to figure out that she'd been offering him the wrong incentive. Money did talk, of course, but not quite the way she'd expected. She'd been so heady with their back and forth and his overwhelming physicality, it had taken her some time to realise she was dangling the wrong carrot.

Having investigated him extensively in the last two days, she should have known the way to flip Edmund Butler was through the Institute. She'd watched a TED talk he'd given where he'd spoken about his brainchild and its work with authority and passion in that deep English baritone. From there she'd fallen down an internet rabbit hole where she'd discovered fascinating papers and case studies and a wealth of vital data from the Institute that had thrust it to the forefront of foetal medicine research.

But that took money. Lots of money.

She had no idea if the Castilonian coffers could cover the eye-watering amount she'd thrown at him but Tavi had told her to do whatever she needed to do and that was what she'd done. It *hadn't* been a test, she knew that—Tavi wasn't her father—but she'd taken it on board as one and if she had to

28   FORBIDDEN FLING WITH THE PRINCESS

pay the sum out of her own substantial bank account, she would.

And she'd done it. Dr Edmund Butler was *in the helicopter,* currently thumbing through the folder of material she'd brought with her—scans, reports, blood results, maternal history notes. And for the first time in forty-eight hours, since the ultrasound performed at the Clínica San Carlos had confirmed there was a serious issue with the babies, Xiomara was breathing easy.

Sure, from her research into the condition she knew there was still a way to go, but with *the* Edmund Butler finally agreeing to accompany her to Castilona, Xiomara knew they were one step closer to ensuring that Tavi and Phoebe's babies would be okay.

'Well, Dr Butler?' she asked when he finally shut the file.

'Ed,' he insisted, looking up for the first time since he'd strapped in and opened the folder. 'Let me at least feel like I'm still on holiday for a little longer.'

Xiomara wasn't sure she could call this guy *Ed.* It seemed so…inadequate. So…*ordinary.* When what he did, what he was going to do for Tavi and Phoebe's babies, was *extra*ordinary.

Not something she ever pictured an *Ed* doing.

For sure, he was doing his best to be that guy. Lying under a palm tree, drinking beer at ten in the morning, his tousled russet hair and scruffy face

AMY ANDREWS 29

so different from the perfectly groomed, cleanly shaven man she'd watched give that fascinating, witty TED talk. But even in holiday mode, dressed for a day lazing on the beach, there was a rangy kind of vitality to him that told her he rarely relaxed.

So yeah, an Ed he was not. Ed*mund*—maybe.

'Well, Ed*mund*?'

A brief sardonic smile touched his mouth but he didn't protest further. He clearly wasn't about to split hairs over *her* choice of name for him, given how he'd pointedly refused to use her title.

'I'll need to do another ultrasound as soon as possible upon landing.'

Xiomara nodded, admiring his businesslike pragmatism. He could still be bitching about his interrupted holiday plans but from the second he'd accepted her proposal he'd morphed from beach bum to internationally renowned foetal medicine specialist. He hadn't even batted an eyelid when she'd told him someone had already been to his room, packed his bag and was transporting it to the helicopter. He'd just nodded, as if he'd been impressed by her efficiency.

'We'll head straight to the clinic when we arrive on Castilona.' She consulted her watch. 'We touch down at the international airport here very soon. The jet is fuelled and ready to go and it's a ten-hour flight home.'

Glancing up, Xiomara found him watching her

30   FORBIDDEN FLING WITH THE PRINCESS

with eyes the colour of her father's most expensive cognac. Eyes a woman could drown in if she had a mind to.

'That puts us on the ground in Castilona at eight in the morning,' she continued. 'They'll be there waiting for us.'

'Good.' He nodded as if he'd expected nothing less. 'This…clinic. Is it any good?'

Xiomara tried not to feel any affront on behalf of her country at the dubiousness in his voice. He was asking a perfectly logical, very professional question. It was a *good* thing. But that didn't stop a stiffness straightening her spine or the frost in her voice. 'Clínica San Carlos is exceptionally well appointed, with the latest in ultrasound technology and a fully appointed operating suite.'

He seemed satisfied with her answer. 'Is it possible to have the images emailed to me?'

'Of course.' Xiomara immediately messaged the clinic's radiologist, her fingers flying over the keyboard of her phone as she asked, 'What can you tell from the notes? It's not…too late?'

Reading that the condition could be fatal for one or both twins without treatment had been sobering but Xiomara had been reassured by the research that they'd caught it early. Still, given that the man beside her had written a lot of the papers she'd read, it would be good to hear it straight from the horse's mouth.

Or *stallion*, in his case.

AMY ANDREWS   31

'From the last report, Phoebe is in stage one. The amniotic fluid parameters are still normal and the donor twin's bladder is still visible so I normally wouldn't intervene at this point, just monitor. There's a fifty-fifty chance that the condition will resolve by itself.'

Xiomara was encouraged by his calm, analytical approach. He was neither laissez faire nor panicked, oozing professionalism and confidence, which put her immediately at ease. 'That's encouraging,' she murmured, placing her phone in her lap.

Another brisk nod. 'The condition most often develops slowly enough that there is time to consider the best course of treatment. But—' his gaze locked with hers, his eyes earnest above the cut of his cheekbones '—things *can* progress quickly, so the… Queen will need to be closely monitored.'

'Of course.' Xiomara doubted that Tavi would let Phoebe out of his sight. Her phone vibrated and she read the message. 'What is your best email, please?' she asked, not bothering to look up from the screen.

Xiomara tapped it in as he relayed it and within a minute she was reading a response. 'Okay… The images should be with you by the time we land.'

'Thank you.'

Placing her phone back in her lap, she picked up the conversation again. 'So…what happens if it's progressed and requires further intervention?'

32 FORBIDDEN FLING WITH THE PRINCESS

'We'll transfer Phoebe to London. I doubt your clinic—as well appointed as it may be—has a fetoscopic laser set up?'

Xiomara smiled sweetly at the sarcasm. 'Not a lot of call for it, no.'

The chopper veered to the right a little and he turned his head to take in the view out of the window as the buildings and runway of the international airport came into view. Xiomara took advantage of his distraction to inspect his profile. His unshaven face did nothing to hide the squareness of his jaw and the jut of his chin. The sensuous half curve of his mouth was just as fascinating as the hollow beneath his prominent cheekbone. A pulse thudded at the side of his neck and, for a ridiculous second, she wondered what it might be like to be the woman who was allowed to lean in and nuzzle him there, feel the flow of his life force on her lips.

What would he smell like there? The sea and sunshine? Like he did now. Or did he usually wear cologne? Something light and woodsy or rich and spicy?

'*Dos minutos, Princesa*,' Xavier said, his hand temporarily closing around the foam tip of the microphone attached to his headset.

Startled by the voice, Xiomara dragged her gaze away from Edmund and smiled her thanks at Xavier, who'd she forgotten was there. Sure, he was very good at being able to melt into the background—despite his size—but security was difficult to ignore, no matter how unobtrusive.

Until today.

The only man she'd been aware of since she'd set foot on that beach was the shirtless one beside her and she didn't even want to think about what that might mean.

'Two minutes,' she repeated in English for Edmund.

Which couldn't come quickly enough. At least on the private jet, they wouldn't be in such close confines.

And he wouldn't be half naked.

Five hours later, Xiomara emerged from the private sleeping quarters of the jet, phone in hand, feeling refreshed. She hadn't thought she'd sleep between her anxiety over the situation with the royal babies and the disturbing presence of Edmund Butler—both on her plane *and* in her head—but she'd been asleep seconds after her head hit the pillow.

She supposed that was a consequence of very little sleep this past forty-eight hours and the overwhelming relief of having achieved what she'd set out to do.

Said achievement was sitting at a square table big enough to accommodate eight large comfortable chairs, two on each side. It was the place where royal business was usually conducted mid-

34   FORBIDDEN FLING WITH THE PRINCESS

flight and, despite his jeans and T-shirt, Edmund looked thoroughly at home, clearly engrossed in whatever was on the screen of a laptop as he tapped away, a cup and saucer near his elbow.

He'd changed into more appropriate clothing once they'd touched down at the airport but if Xiomara had thought it would eliminate the bolt of heat she felt every time he looked her way she'd been sorely mistaken. The denim was soft and worn, hugging his quads and ass like they'd been personally tailored to his measurements. And his graphite-grey T-shirt sat snug across the flat of his abs and taut at the seams of his shoulders.

Xavier, spotting her entrance, stood and greeted her. He was occupying one of the half dozen single armchairs on the opposite side of the aircraft, which could be configured in any number of arrangements.

'Your Royal Highness.' Henri, the flight steward, smiled at her and gave a slight bow. 'I hope you are well rested. Lunch will be served shortly. Can I get you a drink in the meantime?'

Xiomara was aware of Edmund looking over his shoulder at her as she smiled at Henri. 'Coffee, please.'

It was only then that she met his gaze. Their eyes locked as he silently acknowledged her presence and another bolt found its mark, deep and low. 'Would you like a top-up?' she asked, forcing her legs to move towards him.

'Please,' he said with a nod, his eyes moving to Henri. 'Thank you.'

Trying to act nonchalant, Xiomara slid into the chair opposite Edmund, pleased that the distance of the table was between them as she placed her phone down. He shut the lid of the laptop and Xiomara shook her head. 'Please, don't let me interrupt you.' She waved her hand. 'Continue.'

His lips twitched. 'Why, thank you, *Princess*.'

He didn't open his laptop again but he did chuckle and Xiomara realised that had probably sounded like she'd just issued some royal decree. She winced internally—why did this man have her tied in knots? Why was it that she could hold her own with dozens of foreign dignitaries on any given day that would cause the most self-assured person to blanch but in front of this man, despite her outward appearance, she felt completely out of her depth?

Henri approached with their coffees, giving Xiomara a reprieve, a chance to collect herself, and she felt much better equipped to make small talk as he withdrew.

'You changed,' he said.

It was a brief statement of fact but there was nothing brief about the impact of it on her body as his gaze dropped to her shirt then flicked up to her hair, which she'd pulled back into a high ponytail, before returning to her face. His eyes brushed her mouth and she momentarily wished she hadn't switched out the red lipstick for a more sedate shade of pink.

'You're observant.' For someone who'd been photographed *a lot*, Xiomara had, too often, felt invisible in her life.

He shrugged. 'You made quite a statement on the beach.'

Xiomara didn't think that was meant to be a compliment but the fact she'd had an impact on him caused a spike in her pulse. She'd chosen her outfit carefully, applied a thick layer of red lipstick, because she'd *wanted* to make a statement. The man had impressed her—was there anything wrong with wanting to also impress? She couldn't dazzle him with her occupational credentials but at twenty-seven and a paparazzi favourite, Xiomara knew how to get a man's attention.

'Yoga pants are much more comfy to fly in.' Xiomara had been groomed to be a fashion plate and it was fun to have a closet full of amazing designer clothes but, in private, she was an over-sized T-shirt, flip-flops and messy-hair-don't-care kinda girl.

'I will take your word for it,' he said with a slight smile. 'I trust you slept well?'

'Thank you, yes.'

He raised an eyebrow. 'Must be nice to have your own bedroom in the sky.'

It was on the tip of her tongue to invite him into said room for a personal tour so she picked up her cup and took a sip of coffee, swallowing down the urge. If he'd been another man who was causing her this level of sexual titillation, she probably would have. There were, after all, five hours left of the flight and she could think of no better way to pass the time than finding out just how good Edmund Butler was with anatomy.

Also, no place more private—no paparazzi up here.

But the last thing she wanted to do was muddy the waters between them. She needed Edmund for one thing and one thing only. Nothing else was important.

'I'm very lucky,' she conceded.

Her father had always considered wealth and privilege as his due. Her mother, who had mostly raised Xiomara, had taught her the meaning of humility. Thankfully, Mauricio had decided to leave Castilona upon Octavio's ascension, choosing to exile himself in Saudi Arabia. Her mother, Mira, had decided not to leave with him and their divorce was pending.

'Have you flown on a private jet before?'

'Once or twice.' He nodded. 'Short trips for work-related things. Quite different to having one at your constant disposal, I imagine.'

Xiomara couldn't help but think he was judging her right now and that rankled, but she needed to keep her eyes on the prize. 'Royalty does have its privileges.'

'So...this is what a Princess of Castilona does?' He gestured around the interior. 'Flies around in private jets being an...emissary?'

Yeah, okay, he was definitely judging her now. But he was also challenging her again, like he had on the beach and maybe, in lieu of any horizontal action, it would have to do.

'Sometimes.'

'Isn't it chafing being at your cousin's beck and call?'

Folding her arms, Xiomara eyed him. 'No. My cousin *is also my King.* So, when he sends me to get you, I get you. Which is something I'd have thought you, *as a British citizen,* would appreciate.'

'Nah.' He shook his head. 'I'm not much of a fan of unelected figureheads.'

Xiomara blinked. Well, that she hadn't expected. She'd seen pictures of him with different members of the British Royal Family at functions and she'd read several of his research papers that had been funded by various royal trusts. 'You are not a monarchist?'

He chuckled and it puffed whorls of warm air currents in her direction, brushing against her skin, tightening her nipples to achy points. 'Not all Brits are monarchists, Xiomara.'

She supposed not and yet it was easy to believe, looking at picture after picture of him schmoozing with society and aristocracy types, arriving in fancy cars and wearing fancy suits, that he was one of them. Despite knowing his roots to be much humbler.

'Is that because you grew up poor?'

There was a pause as his amber eyes lit with surprise before another chuckle oozed its way across the table. 'I wasn't poor,' he said, his mouth still curved in a generous smile. 'I mean we didn't—' he looked around the interior of the jet '—have our own private plane, but I never wanted for anything. I just *grew up* in poor places.'

'Because your parents worked in the humanitarian sector?'

'Well done, Princess,' he said sardonically, performing a slow clap. 'What else do you know about me?'

He seemed both irritated and intrigued that she'd checked out his background but if he thought she was going to apologise for doing so, then he was going to be severely disappointed. Tavi and Phoebe were *royalty*. Castilona might be largely unknown but that didn't mean she could be laissez faire about their safety.

Folding her arms, Xiomara met his gaze. He was going to be sorry he'd asked.

'You're thirty-four years old, born in Papua New Guinea, the eldest of three children. Your parents are doctors and for the first twelve years of your life you travelled as a family from one crisis spot to the next. You attended international schools or were home tutored during this time of your life.

40   FORBIDDEN FLING WITH THE PRINCESS

Your parents took the family back to the UK in time for you to commence high school. You attended a local comprehensive school in London before receiving a full scholarship to Cambridge to study medicine. After qualifying you specialized in Obstetrics and Gynaecology with a particular interest in fetoscopic techniques. You have three nieces and two nephews. You were engaged briefly ten years ago but have never married and have no dependants. In two weeks you are travelling to Africa for your regular NGO stint.'

Xiomara finally drew breath, their eyes still locked. 'Did I miss anything?'

'Only all the juicy bits in between, but that's—' he lifted a shoulder in a shrug as a small smile lifted the corner of his mouth '—fairly comprehensive.'

It was, although, he was right, had there been more time she would have commissioned a much more detailed report into his background, including information about his ex-fiancée. But it still wouldn't have told her the things she'd found to be the *most* interesting. For example, how thoroughly mesmerizing he was in a pair of floral boardies. How his laugh was warm and deep and welcoming. How the online videos didn't do the smooth baritone of his cultured English accent justice.

And now, of course, those were the intriguing *juicy bits* she suddenly wanted to know *all* about.

'I'm afraid you have me at a disadvantage, Xiomara. Perhaps you can fill me in on what I need to know about you?'

A laugh spilled from her mouth unchecked. The truth was, he didn't need to know anything about her. She was born to be inconsequential. To be in the background. 'I am a princess in a system that privileges male succession. I am...ornamental.' She picked up her cup in salute. 'That is all you need to know about me.'

Xiomara had no idea where that had come from. The truth was, until meeting him, she'd never really questioned her place in life and who she was outside of the de la Rosa dynasty. She'd railed against it from time to time for sure, but had largely accepted it. What little girl didn't grow up harbouring a secret fantasy of being a princess in a palace at some point?

Then this amazingly accomplished guy had come along and in a hot minute had shone a light on her *lack* of accomplishments. Her lack of individual purpose. Her lack of individual *ambition*.

He regarded her for long moments, his amber eyes probing. 'Poor little rich girl, huh?'

Plenty of people back home would have rushed to assure her that her life was full of purpose. That there were many important ways she could represent Castilona and lead a rich and fulfilling life. But not Edmund. There was clearly going to be no sympathy from a guy who must have grown up an eyewitness to enormous poverty and hardship.

42   FORBIDDEN FLING WITH THE PRINCESS

But actually, it felt good that he wasn't up for indulging her pity party. That he was neither invested in—or paid to—kiss princess ass.

She gave a grudging smile from behind the lip of her cup. 'Something like that.'

He eased back in his chair, still holding her gaze. 'You possess an enormous amount of privilege,' he said slowly, as if he was choosing his words carefully. 'I'm sure you could do whatever you set your mind to.'

His bald statement made Xiomara itch all over. She suddenly felt inadequate and passive in her own life. Which made her irritable. At herself, but also at this man she'd known for all of a few hours judging her. It was okay for him; he'd had the kind of freedom she'd never had.

She glanced across at Xavier. A gilded cage was still a cage. 'It's not quite as easy as that.'

'Nothing worthwhile ever is, Xio.'

Her breath hitched at the easy way *Xio* had slipped from his lips. And just like that her irritation melted away in a warm spotlight of intimacy. He wasn't judging her; he was challenging her. Gently. As if he wanted her to succeed.

And he'd called her Xio. She'd been called it before, of course, but not since her father had become Regent and the shortened name hadn't been considered *royal* enough. And not in the way Edmund had said it.

'Apologies.' He grimaced as he shook his head,

his brow furrowing. 'That was very familiar of me. It just…slipped out.'

'No, it's okay.' She shook her head. 'I like it.' Even more so because it had *just slipped out*.

He nodded slowly, a smile hovering on his full lips. 'Xio it is then.'

Everything warmed at the illicit promise of his words until her phone buzzed on the table, startling her back to the here and now. Her pulse was an unsteady echo through her head as she glanced at the screen flashing her cousin's name. *Tavi.* 'I'm sorry, I have to take this.'

'Of course.'

Xiomara stood and crossed to the other end of the plane for some privacy but, as she listened to her cousin, she couldn't help but watch Edmund, his head bowed over his laptop. He'd called her *Xio*. Soft and low. As if they had a secret.

As if they were already lovers…

CHAPTER THREE

SIX HOURS LATER, Edmund was standing in the radiology department of the exceptionally well appointed and clearly very exclusive Clínica San Carlos. The royal jet had touched down less than an hour before and Xavier had whisked both him and the Princess—who had insisted on accompanying him—to the clinic, where they awaited the royal couple.

It was hard to believe twelve hours ago he'd been on a tropical beach in the middle of the Indian Ocean, with barely a building or a soul to be seen. And now here he was, in a small Mediterranean island kingdom boasting an array of expensive yachts in the harbour, hillside vineyards and row upon row of white-washed buildings, their terracotta rooftops a warm, welcoming ochre as they'd made their descent.

On their way to the clinic from the airport they'd passed winding cobblestone lanes where pedestrians dodged mopeds and colour was everywhere. Vibrant splashes of pink and purple bougainvillea had been trained to grow around doorways and across overhead trellises, dappling the light in charming sun-filled alleys. Fat yellow lemons and red geraniums sat in pots on windowsills and terraces.

And then there was the royal palace, which he was looking at now through the window. Wrought iron gates with gilt spikes were guarded by uniformed men with shiny gold buttons. Beyond he could see a large gravelled forecourt dominated by an ornate fountain and then the pale stone walls of the building itself, which was more classically handsome than lavish.

Columns and arches defined the edifice with small balconies in between displaying more vibrant hues from flower boxes alive with pinks and reds, yellows and purples. And the pièce de résistance was the spectacular central dome, drawing the eye upward.

He shook his head—how was this his life?

The only thing he'd ever wanted to be was a doctor and that, like his parents, had been the driving force all his adult life, but he'd never pictured it taking him to places like *this*. He'd assumed he'd follow family tradition into the NGO sphere, and he did spend time every year training doctors in developing countries, but it was funny how life events could lead a person down roads and side alleys they'd never planned on taking.

Like this one to Castilona.

Ed had been to a lot of fancy places in the world but this was a revelation. Despite the fact he'd had his vacation interrupted, he wasn't sad to be here.

46 FORBIDDEN FLING WITH THE PRINCESS

Only sad that he probably wouldn't be here long enough to really explore, and he made a mental note to come back some time.

The door behind him opened and he turned to find a woman entering, followed closely by Xiomara, who had changed yet again. A strappy purple sundress showed off her golden skin as her hair bounced loosely around her head. Her lips were shiny with some kind of pinky gloss, which was nowhere near as bold as the red look from the beach but just as fascinating.

'Good morning, Dr Butler,' the newcomer said, smiling as she crossed the distance between them at a brisk clip. She was petite, fine-featured and smartly dressed in a pinstriped pants suit. Her dark hair was worn back in a sleek chignon and her handshake was as businesslike and professional as the rest of her.

'I'm Dr Lola García,' she said, introducing herself as she held out her hand. 'Director of Clínica San Carlos.'

Like Xiomara, she spoke perfect English with the merest hint of an accent and was an exceptionally striking woman. Attractive, confident, clearly career orientated. And yet he had to force himself to concentrate on her as they shook hands and not let his attention stray to the other woman hovering near the door. A woman who'd practically parachuted into his life, snagging his attention from the get-go.

AMY ANDREWS

For someone whose only career aspiration was *princess* and who was, by her own admission, ornamental, Xiomara had completely confounded him.

'The King and Queen's vehicle has just pulled into the entrance portico,' Xiomara informed him. 'I'll go meet them. We won't be long.'

Ed acknowledged Xiomara's statement with a nod but forced himself to keep his gaze firmly trained on the clinic director. 'Please call me Ed,' he said as Xiomara departed. 'Nice to meet you. It's an amazing set-up you have here.'

He turned around, gesturing with his hand at the state-of-the-art equipment. Frankly, he wouldn't have been surprised to find exactly what he needed to perform the fetoscopic procedure on Queen Phoebe.

'Yes, we are very fortunate to have government support as well as some amazing patrons to keep our doors open.'

'It looks quite exclusive.' The building wasn't anywhere near as grand as the palace but it was hewn from the same pale stone and the frescos decorating the walls in the entrance foyer had reeked of wealth.

'It is. We do a lot of plastic surgery here and many of our clients come from around the world to have procedures done away from prying eyes. But we are just as proud of our public wards that provide free treatment to our population as well

48   FORBIDDEN FLING WITH THE PRINCESS

as our commitment to community health provision in the form of community clinics and other programmes.'

Ed nodded as Lola's eyes sparked with the kind of ferocity and zeal he'd often seen in the NGO sector. She was clearly passionate about her work, which increased her attractiveness even further, and yet it wasn't Lola's voice occupying space inside his brain.

'I'd love a tour after the ultrasound,' he suggested in an effort to concentrate his focus.

'I can definitely arrange that.' She smiled. 'Now—' Lola tipped her head towards the sonogram. 'You've seen the images from two days ago, yes? You know where everything is at?'

'Thank you, yes.'

'I've organized for one of the nurses from the department to be in the room in case you need a hand or need to know where something is.'

'Thank you,' he said again.

As if the nurse had been summoned, she knocked then entered, dressed in brightly patterned scrubs. Close on her heels, a tall man in an expensive suit who looked several years younger than Ed, entered. He had a bronzed complexion and a swathe of dark hair—the archetypal hot young royal made famous by celebrity magazines. He was holding the hand of a blonde woman who looked pale and tired and was clearly very pregnant, a T-shirt stretched over her belly.

AMY ANDREWS

King Octavio and Queen Phoebe, he presumed.

Neither of them looked particularly regal right now, despite the quick curtsey Lola had bestowed. There was a presence about the King, in the way he held himself, that told Ed he was used to sweeping into a room and having everyone's attention. But not today. Today he looked just like any other man whose pregnant wife was experiencing difficulties.

Not a *king*. Not *royal*. Just a husband and a father.

'Dr Butler.' He thrust his hand out as he neared, his voice also only lightly accented. 'Octavio de la Rosa. We appreciate you interrupting your holiday to be here.'

Ed's gaze slid to Xiomara as he shook the King's hand. She'd entered the room behind the royal couple and had stayed there. He'd seen a different side to her since landing in Castilona, the one she'd hinted at on the plane. Stepping out of that helicopter she'd been in the driver's seat, but here she'd taken a definite back seat, seemingly fine with being in her cousin's shadow, actively trying to fade into the bland medical background.

Like some kind of chameleon. Like she could make herself invisible. But *he* saw her.

'Your cousin can be very persuasive,' Ed said. 'You should put her to work at the UN.'

Octavio gave a hint of a smile. 'I may just do that.'

50   FORBIDDEN FLING WITH THE PRINCESS

Ed was pretty sure Xiomara had blushed but then Octavio was gesturing to the woman beside him and his gaze shifted back to the royal couple. 'May I introduce you to my wife. Her Majesty, Queen Phoebe.'

'Oh, please.' The blonde waved away the title with a slender hand, which she then thrust at him to be shaken. 'Just call me Phoebe. Not quite used to all the pomp and ceremony just yet.'

Despite the fact she didn't look Mediterranean, Ed was surprised to hear a twang to her voice. He'd assumed she was English but her accent said Australian? Or maybe New Zealand? He bowed slightly over their clasped hands. 'As you wish.' He smiled at her then, noting how drawn she seemed around her eyes and he reminded himself that, according to her notes, she was only twenty-four. 'How are you doing?'

She let out a heavy breath. 'Okay. I guess.'

Ed nodded. He'd been through this many times with many couples. It was a stressful and worrying time and no less for these two just because they happened to be minor European royalty. And he wouldn't treat them any differently to any other couple. They needed him to be knowledgeable and decisive and give them the best possible outcome—two live babies.

They were looking to *him* for that. They had put themselves and the lives of their unborn babies in his hands and everything he did from this moment forward was about that.

He smiled reassuringly. 'Well, how about we just get right to it so we can see what's happening with the babies and can make a plan?'

'Oh, yes.' She smiled but it was wobbly. 'A plan sounds good.'

Ed asked Phoebe a bunch of pregnancy-related questions as he fired up the sonograph, mostly to distract her because he already knew the answers from her chart. Her husband helped her onto the examination couch and the nurse busied herself getting the Queen settled as Edmund adjusted some settings.

'Do you want the lights out, Dr Butler?' the nurse asked.

'Yes, please,' he said as he grabbed the gel that had been sitting in its heated cradle and turned to Phoebe, who was lying slightly reclined, her shirt pulled up to expose her belly.

Octavio stood on the opposite side of the bed, holding his wife's hand, kissing it lightly and smiling at her confidently as the room darkened. 'Everything's going to be okay, *querida*,' he assured. But there was a tightness around his eyes betraying his own deep concern.

'Okay,' Ed said, his face lit by the light from the screen. 'Let's take a look. Bit of goop.'

He squirted the warmed gel onto the royal belly and used the transducer to distribute it where it was needed. There was always a brief moment before the image appeared on the screen when a litany of worst case scenarios flashed through his mind. Sometimes he had to give parents devastating news and that was the last thing he wanted to do today.

A sliver of light brightened the room and he glanced up from Phoebe's abdomen to find Xiomara slipping out of the door, only to have Phoebe call her back and reach out her other hand. 'Please stay,' she asked. 'I have two of these and I need all the hand holding I can get.' Phoebe glanced at Ed. 'Is it okay if Xiomara stands at the head of the bed? She won't be in your way.'

Ed's eyes met Xiomara's across the dark room and held. He had no doubt the determined young woman who had plucked him off a Seychelles island knew how *not* to be in the way. But, intentional or not, Xiomara de la Rosa was definitely *in his way*, be it at the end of the bed or far across the room.

Every cell in his body was humming right now as she stared at him and he could feel the corresponding hum pulsing off her. As if they were two tuning forks seeking out their perfect *concert A*. Here, not here, she hummed to him. She was in his head. In his thoughts. And tonight, when he slept, she'd probably be in his dreams.

Ed couldn't quite believe anyone could have that

impact in less than twenty-four hours, but here they were.

'Of course,' he murmured, dragging his gaze back to Phoebe. 'There's plenty of room.'

The door clicked shut, extinguishing the slice of light, and Ed busied himself looking at the screen as Xiomara rounded the bed and took up position, putting herself within reaching distance and smack bang in his peripheral vision. Phoebe lifted her arm above her head and Xiomara slipped her hand into Phoebe's with a reassuring smile.

'Okay, then,' Ed said. 'We're all set.'

Returning his gaze to the screen, he manipulated the wand through the gel with one hand while clicking a button with the other to project the picture he could see on his screen onto the larger screen hanging on the wall behind him at the foot of the bed, where everyone's eyes were currently glued. The babies filled the screen, squiggling and kicking around, and Phoebe's soft, '*Oh,*' got lost on a strangled kind of sob.

'What do you know about TTTS?' he asked, directing his question at both Phoebe and Octavio.

'Lola has filled us in and we've been doing some online research,' Octavio murmured, his gaze locked on the screen. 'She did urge us not to but we needed to know everything we could.'

Ed nodded. He too advised his patients not to Dr Google anything but he understood, when all of mankind's knowledge was available at the tap of a key, how tempting that was. And knowledge was, after all, power. The problem was, he had no idea if his patients were finding good information or stuff that was misguided, misleading or just plain wrong.

And then there were the pictures. There were some gruesome images out there which often weren't helpful in emotionally fraught situations.

'To be honest, though,' the King continued, 'it's all been a lot to take in so perhaps if you could go over things again?'

'Of course.' Ed's gaze skimmed Xiomara as it flicked to the sonograph screen, her presence flaring brightly on his internal radar as he tapped some buttons.

'As you know, TTTS occurs when twins are monochorionic, that is, they share a placenta. See—' Ed manipulated the transducer to get the view he wanted, bringing the placenta up on the screen. 'Like that.'

He held the wand in place for a moment or two before continuing.

'Sometimes, in about ten to fifteen percent of twin pregnancies, there is an unequal sharing of blood between the two babies due to blood vessel connections on the surface of the placenta so one twin gets too much blood and the other doesn't get enough.'

AMY ANDREWS   55

'Which means there's too much amniotic fluid and urine for one of the babies, right?' Octavio said.

'Right. Normally, when we ultrasound twins, we give each twin a number—twin one and twin two—but in TTTS we talk about the donor twin, who is the one receiving too little blood, and the recipient twin, who is the one receiving too much blood. Here—' Ed took a few moments to get the best view again '—is the recipient twin. You can see that black bubble? That's the rather large bladder.'

Ed half turned to point to it on the large wall screen behind. 'And here—' more angling of the wand brought up the second baby '—is the donor twin. Whose bladder is still visible.' He again twisted and pointed to the much smaller bubble of fluid.

'And that's a good thing, right?' Phoebe asked.

'Yes.' No urine would have been a major concern. But Ed could see there was a change from the last scan and the computer measurements were already diagnosing a degree of polyhydramnios, or excess amniotic fluid, within the recipient twin's sac. They were still within technical normal limits but the *trend* was a concern.

Once again, his eyes fell on Xiomara, who was watching him closely. Could she tell just by looking at him that he was worried? The way *he* could sense *she* was?

56   FORBIDDEN FLING WITH THE PRINCESS

'But,' he said, returning his attention to the royal couple, 'I think the numbers are moving in the wrong direction.'

A shaky indrawn breath spilled from Phoebe's lips. Octavio's throat bobbed as he lifted his wife's hand to his chest, clasping it tight.

'I want to stress,' Ed said, 'the measurements are still all within the normal range, and you are still in stage one, but they're now at the upper limits of the range.' Ed didn't believe in telling patients bad news without offering them solutions and options. 'It would be my advice to have fetoscopic laser ablation, where we insert a small scope into the uterus with a laser attached, allowing us to destroy the problem vessels. It takes about forty-five minutes and if everything can be organised quickly on this end, I can perform it in London first thing tomorrow.'

'Yes.' Phoebe nodded briskly, sniffling. She glanced at Octavio. 'We'll be able to arrange the jet and security quickly, yes?'

'Yes,' he agreed without hesitation. 'I will organize it and make arrangements to stay at the consulate in Belgravia as soon as we are done here.'

'Good.' Ed nodded. He was pleased that the royal couple were keen to move forward with speed and had the wealth and privilege to do so.

He noticed Phoebe's grip on Xiomara's hand was still quite fierce and he glanced at the woman at the head of the bed. Their eyes met and she mouthed, 'Thank you,' at him, her gaze bright with relief and admiration.

Ed's chest tightened. In his career, he'd received just about every medical accolade there was to be had. And they were great, of course, but it was always the relief and gratitude of patients that meant the most.

Xiomara looking at him as if he'd hung the moon was a whole other thing.

He'd never been one to brag about his accomplishments to impress others—*women* included—instead, he let his success do the talking and, frankly, he was too busy to indulge in ego stroking exercises. But he'd be lying if he didn't admit that impressing the Princess felt pretty damn good.

And he hadn't even done anything yet.

Three hours later, Ed found himself back on the de la Rosa private jet. An emotionally exhausted Phoebe was resting in the bedroom with Octavio by her side. She was bearing up well and trying to stay positive but Ed could see through her façade to a woman who still held very understandable fears for her babies. Octavio had admitted to undertaking online research so Ed figured they'd found a host of stuff there that could give even the most stoic couple nightmares.

It was only natural that either parent would find it hard to relax until after the lasering had been performed and deemed a success.

58   FORBIDDEN FLING WITH THE PRINCESS

Even the procedure itself was a lot for people to grasp. Messing around inside the womb, the amniotic sac of an unborn baby, still somehow seemed like something from science fiction. Not a procedure that had been performed and perfected over the past thirty years on tens of thousands of babies. He could only hope that his experience in this area had help allay some anxieties.

The pilot came over the sound system to announce they were on their way to cruising altitude, that the weather was looking good and they should be touching down at London City Airport in around ninety minutes. Having made all the arrangements for tomorrow's procedure before departing Castilona, all there was for Ed to do was sit back and enjoy the view of the bobbing boats and terracotta rooftops growing smaller and smaller as the plane steadily lifted.

'It's just as pretty from the air, isn't it?'

Ed smiled to himself at the husky edge to the slightly accented English before turning away from the window to find her taking the seat opposite him in what was her fourth outfit since they'd met—red capri pants and an oversized green button-down shirt. He hadn't been surprised to find Xiomara would be accompanying the royal couple. She seemed very close to her cousin and his wife, and it was only natural that Phoebe wanted to have as much support as she could get.

He'd also been secretly pleased. The thought of

flying away and never seeing her again had made his blood itch in a way that was both scintillating and disturbing. Sitting opposite her as they stared at each other, their attraction *humming* away, only confirmed it. He wanted her. Deeply, wholly, shamelessly.

He wanted her like he'd never wanted another woman.

But there was also something very *virgin princess in a tower* about her that made him wary. When he'd first met her, there'd been nothing demure about her at all as she'd bartered for his services like she'd grown up in a Turkish bazaar. And then they'd arrived in Castilona and she'd morphed into that person she'd told him about on the plane—ornamental.

The dichotomy both intrigued and confused him. Part of him wanted to storm the walls and climb the tower to rescue that woman that had whisked him away in a helicopter, and yet the other part of him could see that the door wasn't locked. She was *choosing* to stay.

As if the tower was as much a construct of her mind as it was made of bricks and mortar.

Ed had no idea what that meant, only that it probably wasn't wise to find out. She was, after all, a princess who did…*princessy* stuff about a million miles away from his world. But in twenty-four hours she'd completely blindsided him and he

60 FORBIDDEN FLING WITH THE PRINCESS

knew if he didn't get to sink his hand into her hair and kiss her soon he might just go mad.

'It is,' he said, his gaze drifting over that amazing halo of curly hair, the arch of a cheekbone, the curve of her bottom lip, the graceful line of her throat, the swell of her cleavage nicely framed by the V-neck of the shirt. 'I will have to return one day to explore it more.'

Ed hadn't meant anything sexual—not consciously anyway—by his comment but he could tell by the slight up-tilt of her mouth and the amused lift of her eyebrow that she'd taken it that way. 'Please do let us know should you ever return. You are welcome to stay at the palace as our special guest at any time.'

Ed chuckled. *Please do let us know.* Looked like a pin-up girl, spoke like a princess. 'I was thinking more like a moped and a tent.'

She laughed then. '*You* know how to pitch a tent?'

It was Ed's turn to lift an eyebrow. Had she deliberately used that phrase? Her English was certainly good enough to grasp innuendo so was she…flirting with him? With three black-booted security guards, a steward and two other palace staff within hearing distance?

Not very virgin-princess-in-a-tower.

Nor was the way she'd crossed her leg, a sparkly flip-flop dangling off her equally sparkly toes. Maybe the combined palpable relief of everyone on board at being on the way to London was loosening her up a little.

'I've pitched lots of tents in my life,' he parried. 'Only way to travel.'

'This from the man I found at an exclusive resort in the Seychelles?'

'Well.' He lifted a shoulder. 'It's been a long time since I've had a proper holiday and I'm about to spend four weeks visiting places that aren't known for their indoor plumbing. What is money for if not to treat oneself every now and then?'

She didn't answer the question, just tilted her head and asked, 'Why so long?'

'Life has been completely hectic. Between patients and research and getting the Institute up and running and travelling to symposiums and conferences and guest lecturing and doing some NGO work, I looked up and suddenly it's been five years.'

He'd thrived on his schedule though, the professional drive he always felt pushing him ever onwards. But his family and friends had been begging him to take a break or risk burning himself out so he'd finally agreed to stop their nagging.

'And then a princess from a faraway land jumps out of a helicopter and takes that away from you too.'

She said it in an utterly self-deprecating way, leaving Ed completely charmed. He smiled. 'A princess in a silver dress.'

He was pretty sure that dress would be the last thing he thought about as he left this world.

Her cheeks pinked up as her gaze moved to the window, staring out of it as if there was something extra fascinating about the endless blue nothing.

'What about you?' he asked. 'I don't suppose Princess Xiomara of the royal house de la Rosa has ever camped out anywhere.'

Returning her attention to him, her expression turned affronted in the most aristocratic of ways, her pink cheeks changing from embarrassed to indignant. 'I've camped before. I can rough it.'

Ed threw back his head and laughed, ignoring her indignant, imperious expression.

'What?' she demanded.

'That—' he gestured to her clothes '—is the fourth outfit I've seen you in and I've only known you twenty-four hours.'

'You seemed to be obsessed with the clothes I wear, Edmund.'

Not as obsessed as he was at seeing her out of them… But, *nope*. Do *not* go there! Time to get the conversation back on track, Ed*mund*. 'So…when is the best time to visit Castilona?'

She smiled as if she knew very well what he was doing, but thankfully she took the bait. 'Any time during summer, but in two weeks the Fiesta del Vino de Verano begins and goes on for the entire month of August.'

Ed narrowed his eyes as he tried to translate

from his school-boy Spanish. 'Sounds like there's wine in there somewhere?'

'You are correct. Festival of the summer wine.'

'My kind of festival.'

She tilted her head to the side, another smile hovering on her mouth. 'I thought British men liked beer?'

'I like beer well enough, but for savouring? Can't beat a glass of wine.'

'Well, you should definitely visit during August. All the cafés and restaurants feature the local vintages, every cellar door on the island puts on speciality menus, shops and houses and piazzas are decorated in grapes and vines and it all culminates on the last Sunday of the month with the ritual grape crushing in the *Plaza Centrale,* which is full of half barrels where locals and tourists alike can jump in and stomp grapes with their feet.'

'Sounds like fun.'

She nodded. 'It is.' Their gazes locked and held for a long moment and he wasn't sure if she *wanted* to convey that she was up for some fun but she most certainly *was* and the hum between them pulsed like a living entity, swirling and tugging.

'Your Royal Highness?' the steward interrupted, completely oblivious to the crackle between them, although God knew how. The air currents were so charged it surely had to be a hazard having them both on this aircraft. 'Queen Phoebe is asking for you.'

64   FORBIDDEN FLING WITH THE PRINCESS

'Thank you.' She bestowed a demure smile on the steward as she unbuckled. 'Will you excuse me, Dr Butler?' she asked, all prim and polite and virgin princess, as if she hadn't just communicated all kinds of possibilities with those endlessly fascinating green eyes.

Ed nodded just as politely. 'Of course... *Xio*.' Two could play at that game.

He didn't miss the slight falter in her step as she walked away.

CHAPTER FOUR

'Okay, Phoebe, we're all set,' Ed announced from behind his mask.

He'd performed another ultrasound this morning when the royal couple had presented themselves at the hospital after a night in their apartment situated within the grounds of the Castilonian consulate in Belgravia. It had confirmed that the TTTS had progressed to stage two, with the donor twin's bladder having no visible urine, and the decision to go ahead and ablate was the correct one.

'How are you guys doing back there?' He peeped over the drape that had been erected between the head of the bed and Phoebe's bared, draped abdomen.

'Hmm, good,' Phoebe murmured sleepily. 'Nervous but whatever you gave me has helped.'

Grace Adams, the anesthetist, had administered some light sedation along with placing an epidural. The procedure was minimally invasive and not felt by mother or babies, but it was important Phoebe stayed still throughout and that she was the most relaxed she could possibly be given the high anxiety of the situation.

Being gowned and gloved in an operating theatre, beneath the overhead lights, surrounded by people dressed exactly as he was and a host of medical equipment he knew inside out was second nature to Ed. This was where he felt most at home. He knew what had to be done and he was good at his job. Standing here, about to wipe some prep over Phoebe's exposed belly, he did so with the supreme confidence of a man who was the best in his field.

But he was always cognizant of how different it was on the other side of that drape.

'We give good drugs here,' Grace said, a smile in her voice as she patted Phoebe's shoulder.

Ed glanced at Octavio who, even in scrubs, paper hat and a mask managed to look regal. 'How you doing?'

He nodded but there was a tightness around his eyes. 'I'll be better when it's all over.'

'And that's my cue,' Ed said good-naturedly. 'All right, let's begin.'

The rhythm of the theatre took over as Ed's focus narrowed. There was the blip of Phoebe's heart rate on the monitor but otherwise it was just the low murmur of necessary instructions and discussion as instruments were asked for and Ed's colleague positioned the ultrasound transducer, which would guide the entry of the fetoscope into the recipient twin's amniotic sac.

'Okay, I'm putting the scope in now.'

Ed usually narrated throughout any procedure

where the patient was awake, to keep them informed and help ease anxiety. An operating theatre was a highly medicalized environment which could be overwhelming to lay people already stressed enough.

Puncturing the skin, Ed manoeuvred the instrument under the guidance of the ultrasound. The fetoscope was long and flexible, less than four millimeters in diameter but packed with technology. Within the slender package there was a camera, a suction tube and the laser.

'And we're in,' he said as the watery world of the royal babies came to life on the screen at the foot of the operating table.

Ed took a second as he usually did to just marvel at the miracle of it all. It was a sight few ever got to see, the gentle float of a foetus inside the womb, tiny but perfectly formed. Toes and fingers, nose and lips and a network of spindly looking vessels visible beneath the translucent skin.

'Just navigating to the placenta now.'

Manipulating the scope from the outside, Ed watched the screen as the smooth ruddy landscape of the placenta came into view. More functional than attractive, it was nonetheless a marvel of evolution, its tributaries of red and blue supplying everything a baby needed to grow and develop.

'Okay, found the cord insertion site—we'll spend some time now mapping the surface,' Ed informed them. 'We identify all the vessels con-

68   FORBIDDEN FLING WITH THE PRINCESS

necting the twins first, then we seal them off with the laser.'

Ed and the team worked in tandem, methodically pinpointing where he'd need to treat. Given the narrow field of vision afforded by the scope, this was often the longest part of the procedure but they had to be thorough.

Satisfied that they'd found the problematic connections, Ed prepared to progress to the next stage. 'Right, now on to the *Star Wars* part,' he joked. 'All good your end, Grace?'

Grace eyed the monitor and the steady blip of Phoebe's pulse. 'Yep, all good.'

For the next ten minutes, Ed systematically ablated each of the vessels he'd noted on his reconnaissance, the laser flaring bright on the screen as it obliterated each interconnected pathway.

After checking and rechecking that they'd got them all, he announced, 'We're done.'

'It's all good? You're happy with it?' Phoebe asked, still sounding a little spacey but clearly needing the reassurance.

'Very happy,' Ed said with the confidence of having performed the procedure countless times. 'As we discussed earlier, I'm just going to reduce some of the amniotic fluid from around this little one and then we're done.'

Excess amniotic fluid increased the chances of premature membrane rupture and pre-term birth and he was here to give the babies the best possible outcomes. Twins were often born slightly premature anyway but the object here was to ensure the babies got as far advanced in their gestation as possible before making their entries into the world.

'It's good, *querida,* it's good,' Ed heard Octavio murmur to his wife.

Fifteen minutes later, Phoebe was being wheeled back to her room accompanied by her husband as Ed de-gowned, tossing it into a bag, the frigid climes of the OR fresh on his skin.

'So, are you going back to the Seychelles?' Grace asked as she removed her mask and disposed of it in the bin.

'Nah, think I'll stick around now I'm back.'

He should return, he knew. He still had nine days booked and paid for. But the de la Rosas would be staying on in London for the next week as a precaution and considering how much money they were donating to the Institute, the least he could do was stick around and be on hand in case any complications arose.

Not that he was expecting any but, as with any procedure, there were risks, which he'd already discussed thoroughly with Octavio and Phoebe.

He could certainly do the follow-up ultrasounds. They didn't need to be performed by him—a sonographer could easily do them—but he knew Phoebe and Octavio would appreciate him taking a personal hand in their case. He didn't think for a moment that they thought their donation bought

70   FORBIDDEN FLING WITH THE PRINCESS

them special treatment but, given that he was still on vacation and he had no patient load or anything else on his plate, he was happy to give them the gold star treatment.

And yes, okay, the fact he might get to see more of Xiomara wasn't exactly a hardship. He assumed that as long as the royal couple were in London, she'd be in London too, which opened up a lot of possibilities.

'Staycation, huh?'

'Yup.' Sure. Why not?

He lived in one of the world's most popular tourist spots, why not noodle around his own city? Or take one of the many easy daytrips that could be had from the nation's capital.

Maybe even invite a certain princess along for the ride?

Xiomara's chest gave a funny little leap at the knock on the door. She was sitting in the chair next to Phoebe's bed. Phoebe hadn't stopped smiling since they'd arrived back at the luxuriously appointed private suite. Neither had Tavi. It was such a relief seeing the weight lifted from their shoulders. It had only been four days since the terrible ultrasound result but it had felt like a month.

Not that it mattered now because everything was going to be okay and that was all thanks to Edmund Butler, who was standing on the other side of the door.

AMY ANDREWS 71

Xiomara knew it was him.

She could *feel* it in that way she'd been aware of him since setting foot on the Seychelles, a storm in her belly as chaotic as the sand that had blown around her from the helicopter rotors.

'I'll get it,' she said, leaping up, waving Tavi back into his seat.

Xiomara forced herself to cross the room sedately like a princess who'd undertaken years of deportment and posture lessons. Not a giddy teenager giving into the demands of her tripping pulse.

Drawing in a steadying breath she opened the door, but it whooshed out of her as Edmund loomed there, taking up all the space in a set of scrubs.

Hell, it took all of her fortitude not to swoon in a heap at his feet.

Dios! A man should not look that good in what were essentially blue pyjamas. Even if they did hug him to perfection.

'*Xio,*' he greeted as his gaze roved over her face and hair and neck and, God help her, lower.

She'd dressed this morning in her favourite form-fitting, V-neck pink T-shirt with a glittery tiara stamped across the front, teaming it with a flowy, layered skirt of soft tulle that hid a multitude of sins and flirted with her ankles. For comfort, she'd told herself. Nothing stiff or formal or fancy for a long day sitting in the hospital keeping Phoebe company.

72   FORBIDDEN FLING WITH THE PRINCESS

But in truth, she'd worn it for him, this man who seemed to have such a preoccupation with her clothes. Because she'd wanted him to look at her as he was now, his gaze brushing her neck and the swell of her breasts that were spilling out of satiny demi-cups to form a pillowy cleavage. She'd wanted to see his amber eyes darkening to a predatory tawny.

She'd wanted him to look at her as if she wasn't some pretty, unattainable, untouchable princess on a pedestal but as if she was a woman who knew her own power. A woman who craved his touch.

She might be a little younger than him but she was no virgin.

And in those long beats she totally forgot herself and their surroundings. And that two of the palace security detail were witnessing this mutual display of ogling that violated all kinds of royal protocols. Commoners should never look upon a royal princess with such unbridled lust. And a princess should definitely not be wondering how easy it was to get a man out of a pair of scrubs.

Were there snaps on those trousers or a drawstring?

Suddenly breathless at the direction of her thoughts and stunning lack of royal decorum, Xiomara gave herself a mental shake. *Do not mentally undress world-famous doctor with the King and Queen of Castilona mere metres away.*

'Dr Butler,' she murmured, clearing her throat as she stepped aside. 'Do come in.'

He grinned at her then, filthy and wicked, as if he could read every one of the dirty thoughts behind her demure royal façade and was going to take great pleasure in making her say each one of them out loud to him when he finally got her into his bed.

Because Xiomara knew, without a shadow of a doubt, that was exactly where this was heading.

'Thank you, *Princess.*'

His voice was low as pitch and as he brushed past her, the sleeve of his scrubs whispering over her décolletage. Xiomara's belly flipped and muscles deep inside squeezed tight.

'Ed.' Tavi rose and met the doctor halfway, reaching out his hand to shake it.

Xiomara watched as the man she regarded most in the world—her beloved cousin, her monarch— also violated royal protocol and pulled the good doctor into a brief, hard bearhug then apologised for it as he let go.

'Sorry,' he said, clearly surprised and possibly a little embarrassed at his spontaneity. 'I didn't plan on doing that.'

Edmund laughed and gave the royal shoulder a brief squeeze of reassurance. 'It's fine,' he dismissed. 'Happens all the time.'

'You're lucky I'm not up to standing yet or you'd have one from me, too,' Phoebe chimed in.

74   FORBIDDEN FLING WITH THE PRINCESS

Another laugh from Edmund as he switched his attention to Phoebe. 'How are you feeling?'

'Good. Relieved. Happy.' She held out her hand. 'Thank you again.'

Ed took three paces to the bed and took her outstretched hand, enfolding it in both of his, patting it absently. 'Happy to oblige.'

'You've been a godsend,' she said. 'We're so lucky Xiomara was able to locate you. I don't know what I'd do without her.'

Xiomara held her breath as Edmund glanced across at her, those tawny eyes roving over her again as if they were the only people in the room. His gaze touched *everywhere,* igniting a series of sparks beneath her skin and when it lingered briefly on the glittery tiara stamped across her breasts her nipples hardened shamelessly.

'You are indeed,' he murmured. Then he turned back to Phoebe, looking from her to Tavi and back to her again. 'Do either of you have any questions?'

'What time in the morning will you do the ultrasound?' Phoebe asked, diving straight in.

'I'm normally doing rounds by seven-thirty, but I could come earlier if you'd like?'

'Oh, no.' She shook her head. 'You've been too kind already. Whenever you'd normally get here is perfectly fine.'

Ed chuckled then and Xiomara felt it from across the room like a subterranean kind of rumble working up through her toes and her calves and her thighs, setting up camp right between her legs. A man's laugh should not have such a potent effect on a woman's body.

This sexual attraction was fast veering out of control.

'How about I get here at six? I know you'll be anxious until you can actually see the procedure has worked and I don't mind.'

Phoebe pulled her bottom lip between her teeth and Xiomara could see she was clearly torn between needing confirmation the procedure was a success and being demanding or unreasonable. 'We've already asked so much of you.'

Another laugh. 'I'm pretty sure I can get my ass out of bed a little earlier tomorrow for a million-pound donation.'

Tavi hadn't batted an eyelid when Xiomara had informed him what she'd offered. She'd shown her cousin the information she'd gathered on the Institute and he'd been thoroughly impressed by Edmund's brainchild.

'Given the circles we move in,' Tavi said, 'I don't think it'll be the last money finding its way into the Institute's coffers.'

'Thank you.' Ed inclined his head slightly. 'That's very generous. Research doesn't come cheap.'

'It does not,' the monarch agreed.

'Okay, so, six it is.' Ed smiled at the couple. 'As

76   FORBIDDEN FLING WITH THE PRINCESS

discussed, if all is well with the ultrasound—' a sudden crease in Phoebe's forehead caused him to falter '—which I'm fully expecting it to be,' he reassured with a smile, 'you can return to your lodgings in Belgravia. I'll do a follow-up ultrasound on day two and day three as well. Then another at day seven. You can return to Castilona after that and continue with weekly ultrasounds there. And of course I will be at the end of a phone at all times if you need me.'

Phoebe smiled gratefully, the crease between her eyes ironed out. 'Thank you.'

He nodded. 'Get some rest. You look like you have some catching up to do.'

'She does,' Tavi said, dropping a kiss on the back of his wife's hand.

'You do too, Tavi,' Xiomara said.

Her cousin had been keeping up a stoic façade, bolstering Phoebe and taking all her fears and anxieties onto his big shoulders. But she knew him too well, could see beyond the veneer to how exhausted he was from worry and lack of sleep.

Xiomara swore he'd sprouted grey hairs overnight.

'I will,' he said. 'I just have a few things that need my attention today then I can relax.'

A round table situated near the window in the suite had a sheaf of papers and a laptop set up and ready to go. Tavi had been neglecting matters of state but royal business didn't stop for anything. Now, however, with Phoebe's procedure done and things looking good, he would be able to tackle the backlog. Especially with Xiomara here to keep Phoebe company.

'What are your plans for the day?' Phoebe enquired. 'I'm very conscious we've interrupted your holiday, and we're so sorry for that.'

'Do you know,' Edmund said, a smile playing on his mouth, 'I have a Netflix account I barely ever use and I've never watched *The Crown*. I hear it's quite good.'

Tavi and Phoebe laughed. 'Back when I was plain old Phoebe James from New Zealand, I adored it. Loved all the glitz and glamour,' she confessed. 'Had I known back then I was going to be a *queen* one day, I might have taken some notes.'

'I guess that's a bit of a head spin?'

Phoebe bugged her eyes. 'You have no idea. But—' she smiled at Tavi as her hand slid on her pregnant belly '—I wouldn't want to be anywhere else.'

Xiomara envied Phoebe. She understood it was a strange new world to be thrust into as an adult but to have had all those years of being a normal person sounded like bliss to her.

'Right, well.' Edmund straightened. 'I'll leave you to rest and I'll see you both bright and early

78　FORBIDDEN FLING WITH THE PRINCESS

tomorrow morning.' Glancing at Tavi, he said, 'You have my number if you have any concerns.'

Tavi stood and shook hands again. 'Thank you, yes.'

Completely absorbed in the fact Edmund was about to walk out of the room and how very much she didn't want him to, it took Xiomara a beat or two to realise that the door had opened abruptly and that Xavier had entered, an expression of urgency on his face.

'Apologies, Your Majesties, Your Royal Highness,' he said with a bow. Then he spoke quietly to Tavi in Spanish. Tavi muttered a curse under his breath that didn't need any interpretation.

Curse words had the same cadence in any language.

'What?' Phoebe asked, her eyes widening as she looked from her husband to the bodyguard who had crossed to the windows and was pulling the curtains closed.

'There's some paparazzi outside the main entrance,' Xiomara translated for Phoebe, her stomach sinking.

'Oh.' Phoebe sighed. 'How on earth did they know about this?'

Who knew how the vultures ever found out these things? Whilst some people courted that kind of attention, Xiomara never had. Neither had Tavi. But it always seemed to find them. Royal fever always ran hot with the paparazzi, and with Tavi and

Phoebe's snap wedding and now the twins, it had stepped up a notch, bringing with it the inevitable conjecture—would Princess Xiomara be next?

Tabloid interest in her had always been strong, especially during the years of her father's regency. Speculation about any man she was ever seen with seemed to get more and more intense and pictures of Xiomara—with or without a man—could go for a pretty penny. Which made it difficult to keep her private life private. She was largely left alone on Castilona but in Europe there was always some pap or other on her tail.

Tavi sighed. 'I guess we'll have to make a statement.'

Advised by the department of royal protocol, Tavi and Phoebe hadn't released any information about their trip to London, hoping to keep their private details private. It was a difficult line to walk, Xiomara knew, working out what was up for public consumption and what was not. As the monarchs of Castilona, a lot of their life was not their own—that was just a fact.

But Tavi had wanted to give them some breathing space should the news in London not be good. Had it been a different outcome today, he'd wanted to be able to process that with Phoebe without the entire world wanting a piece of them. With paps at the door, however, things could easily get out of hand. Speculation would mount and soon grow rife if they didn't try to control the message.

80   FORBIDDEN FLING WITH THE PRINCESS

'Can we wait till after the ultrasound tomorrow?' Phoebe asked, worrying her bottom lip. She was new to the tabloid circus and already not a fan.

'Of course, *querida*.' Tavi smiled at her. 'I'll speak with my office about it and get them to work on some language.'

Phoebe nodded as Xavier addressed Edmund. 'Dr Butler, we can accompany you out the back entrance if you like?'

'Oh...' He frowned. 'No, it's fine,' he dismissed. 'I doubt the paparazzi are going to be interested in me and my car's out front.'

Xavier inclined his head. 'As you wish.'

He departed the room and, with another quick goodbye, Ed followed. Xiomara tracked his progress—she couldn't not—his scrubs pulling taut around his quads with each long stride. Pausing at the door, his gaze slid briefly to her, lingering on her mouth. It was the merest of seconds but Xiomara's breath hitched, the air in her lungs suddenly turning to liquid heat.

Then he was gone, the door clicking shut behind him, leaving Xiomara to contemplate how many more hours she'd have to wait before she could politely dismiss herself and go to him.

CHAPTER FIVE

SEVEN HOURS. IT took Xiomara seven hours to extricate herself from the hospital. She didn't mind—not *much*, anyway. Tavi's work took longer than expected and as she and Phoebe had become fast friends this year, keeping her company while her husband worked was easy enough.

But she was buzzing now as she stepped out of the lift on Edmund's floor, flanked by her royal protection. Buzzing with pent-up energy from being cooped up in a room all day. Buzzing from the bare-knuckle ride through London traffic to lose the paps that had been waiting at the back entrance with their ridiculous telephoto lenses and mopeds. Buzzing with banked desire, the embers smouldering away deep inside her belly, waiting to roar to life once again.

Buzzing for *him*. For Edmund.

She had no idea how he would feel about her turning up on his doorstep and for a horrible moment she was gripped with uncertainty. What if this was all one-sided and she was so in lust she'd been misreading his signals? What if he flirted with every woman who crossed his path? What

82   FORBIDDEN FLING WITH THE PRINCESS

if right at this very moment he was Netflix *and chilling* with another woman?

Had switching out her pink gloss for red lipstick in the car been a mistake?

Her steps faltered but it was too late, they were at his door and Xavier was knocking and it was opening and there he stood, a T-shirt hugging the contours of his chest, shorts that hit just above his knee moulding the lean musculature of his legs, his feet bare. She was beginning to realise this man looked good in anything.

She had no doubt he'd look just as good in nothing.

His eyes widened a little in surprise but then they took a turn over her body that was possibly more pornographic than it had been earlier in the day, roving everywhere, hot and restless and thorough, lingering on the tiara stamped across her breasts, leaving Xiomara in little doubt she *had not* misread his signals.

'Princess,' he murmured as his gaze returned to her face. 'I don't recall giving you my address.'

His voice was low but brimming with an indulgent kind of humour, curving his lips, drawing her gaze to them like moth to flame. 'You didn't.' She raised her eyes to meet his. 'May I come in?' For she would surely die if she didn't kiss him in the next minute.

His gaze flicked to the two men standing behind her. 'Will they be staying? Should I put out snacks?'

Xiomara smiled at his easy humour. It would have been fair for Edmund to be annoyed at her invasion of his privacy. As well as arriving unannounced on his doorstep with two guys—the confirmed presence of the paparazzi had dictated more manpower—who regarded him as a potential threat to their protectee. The fact that he wasn't, that he was almost amused by it, cranked up his sex appeal another notch.

'They just need to check out your apartment then they'll leave.'

'Do you mind, Dr Butler?' Xavier asked.

Edmund didn't say anything for a beat, he just held her gaze before sliding his hand up the doorframe, anchoring his fingers over the top and stepping aside. Carlos stayed behind in the corridor as Xavier entered the apartment and there they stood, him and her, just looking at each other, gazes locked, as a beefy guy in black moved around behind Edmund and another stood sentinel behind her.

But her security might as well not have been there for all Xiomara noticed, her world narrowed down to the man directly in front of her, staring at her with heat and intent, every deliciously wicked thought going through his head right there in his amber eyes for her to see. Any temporary doubts

84   FORBIDDEN FLING WITH THE PRINCESS

she might have had about a one-sided desire completely obliterated.

He wanted her. As much as she wanted him.

Her pulse tripped like crazy, a tiny hammer at her temples and throat. Her nipples poked hard as diamonds against the confines of her bra. An ache, hot and needy, flared between her legs and it was all Xiomara could do to not squeeze her thighs together.

'All clear,' Xavier announced as he exited the apartment. 'Call us when you're ready to come home later.'

His gaze still locked on her, Edmund said, 'She'll be staying here tonight.'

Xavier didn't miss a beat. 'Call us if you go out.' It wasn't his role to judge Xiomara's actions, just to ensure she was adequately protected and his absolute discretion went without saying.

Amber eyes darkened to tawny. 'We're not going anywhere.'

Xiomara did squeeze her thighs together then as a surge of heat cranked up the ache. The possessiveness of those two statements was absolute. He hadn't asked, he hadn't suggested. Royal princess or not, she was staying the night and they were going nowhere. The squeeze only worsened the situation however and she almost moaned at the deliciously torturous sensation rolling through her pelvic floor.

'Your Royal Highness,' Xavier said as he and Carlos departed.

Xiomara barely registered their departure, her eyes only on Edmund as his hand dropped from the door and he took a step back. Every cell in her body quivering in a state of supreme excitability, Xiomara took a step forward, crossing the threshold. 'I'm sorry,' she said, her voice husky and as quivery as everything else. 'I should have checked you were okay with this.'

He retreated another step, allowing her to advance, but as soon as she cleared the doorway he reached for her, snagging her waist with one hand as he batted the door shut with the other.

'What took you so bloody long?' he growled.

Caging her hips with his hands, he walked her two paces to the wall and pinned her there with one big thigh between her legs and all ten fingers thrusting into her hair as his mouth crashed down on hers.

Dios, yes.

Xiomara's heart rate spiked as her senses exploded with the smell and the taste and the feel of him coming at her from every direction. The heat of his mouth, the rub of his chest against the hard, tight points of her nipples, the urgent press of his thigh causing the most insane friction at the apex of her thighs. The hot, insistent probe of his tongue had her clutching at his shirt, causing the strap from her handbag to slide off her shoulder and fall to the floor.

Not that she noticed as she opened to him, whimpering into his mouth, ploughing her hand into his hair as the kiss deepened. The sound of his harsh breath roared like a stadium in her head and the timbre of his low groan ruffled the hairs on her nape and all she could think was—*yes.*

This.

She'd been thinking about *this* all day. Hell, she'd been thinking about it since the moment she'd spotted him through a haze of white sand on that beach. And it had already exceeded her expectations. Edmund Butler didn't kiss her like she was a princess. Like he was trying to impress her or win her favour. Like she was special.

He kissed her like she was a woman.

Everything felt hot, her blood itched and her lungs were on fire and she never wanted it to end. His hand slid to her ass, lifting her leg, pressing her inner thigh to the outside of his hip, jamming his leg in higher and harder, angling everything just right, leveraging that space between her legs like he and he alone knew exactly how to conquer it.

Moving restlessly against the thick bulk of his quad, Xiomara gasped as muscles deep and low shuddered at the action and she knew she'd die if he wasn't inside her soon.

'Edmund…' she panted against his mouth, her hands sliding to his belly and the snap of his shorts as the need to touch him consumed her. 'Please. I need you…right now…'

Which turned out to be the wrong thing to say as he dragged his mouth from hers, his tawny gaze suddenly cloudy like he was coming out of a daze. 'Jesus, *Xio*.' He groaned as he pressed his forehead to hers, their ragged breathing intermingling. 'I don't usually jump on women the second they walk through my door.' He pulled away slightly to look into her eyes. 'We should slow down.'

Xiomara's brain wasn't exactly in an analytical space right now so she had to force herself to concentrate on his words as her fingers stilled at his fly. Slow down?

She *did not* want to slow down.

If this was some kind of courtship, she wouldn't be starting like this. She *didn't* do this. She'd want to date and get to know him more. Make out a little. Build to this moment. But this wasn't that. Because in one week she'd go back to Castilona and royal life and he'd be heading to Africa to do his thing. This was a moment snatched out of time. A bubble of opportunity.

And she'd be foolish not to take what was on offer.

Sure, the man fascinated her and she liked him very much but it wasn't like they could ever be a thing. He had an amazing career. People who needed and depended on him and his skills and talents. He was driven, she knew that about him as sure as she knew the sun would rise in the east tomorrow. Why would he give that up to be her glorified handbag as she undertook her royal duties?

This was all they could have.

'No.' Xiomara hooked her leg around the back of his thigh. 'I came here for this.'

He chuckled. 'Xiomara Maria Fernanda de la Rosa, I'm shocked.'

Pfft. As if. 'You don't like direct?'

'I like direct very much.' To demonstrate his appreciation, he hitched her higher against the wall, his thigh grinding into all the heat and wet between her legs. 'Tell me how you want it.'

'Here.' Xiomara was proud of how strong her voice sounded when the grind of his thigh was scrambling her brain and melting her insides, inching her closer to orgasm. 'Against this wall.'

One black eyebrow winged upwards. 'Wouldn't the royal Princess prefer a bed?'

'No.' Too many men treated her like a princess. 'I don't need a feather bed or a gilt frame.' Her fingers made short work of his fly, dragging it down. 'I don't need pampering or pretty words.'

Locking her eyes on his, she slid her hand inside, brushing against the long, hard length of him through the barrier of his underwear. The loud suck of his breath was as dizzying as the steady, intimate rub of his thigh.

'Just you and me and this.'

Reaching inside his underwear, Xiomara freed

his erection, pressing her mouth to his as she wrapped her hand around his girth, his deep, guttural grunt sweet on her tongue.

He didn't need any more direction after that, his hand smoothing up her torso, taking her shirt up as well. Up, up, all the way up until he was breaking the kiss and her hold on him to pull it over her head, exposing the demi-cup of champagne-coloured satin that lifted and presented her breasts, the mocha of her areolas peeping out from under the darker lace trim.

'Bloody hell,' he whispered, staring at them like they were the holy grail of mammary glands. 'Is it disrespectful of me to say *great tits*, Princess?'

Xiomara supposed it was, but she liked the way he disrespected her, how he looked at her like he couldn't get enough and he didn't wait for an answer anyway, his hands lowering to peel down the cups, his head lowering to tongue the swell of her cleavage.

She whimpered as the hot, wet heat of his mouth closed over an achingly taut nipple, her back arching as the scruff of his whiskers scraped in all the *good* ways. Twisting a hand into the hair at his nape, Xiomara held him there as her other hand returned to his shorts, grasping him firmly again, revelling in the thick, blunt heaviness of him. He grunted at the play of her fingers as he pulled the other nipple into his mouth, swirling his tongue around it, then sucking hard, shooting a flaming

90 FORBIDDEN FLING WITH THE PRINCESS

arrow of desire straight to the point where she was now shamelessly rutting against his thigh.

She didn't need evidence to know she was wet and ready for him, she could feel the slipperiness between her legs, smell the heady odour of her arousal. Nor did she have to be an expert to know that things were escalating quickly, sparks firing behind her belly button and the base of her spine, nerve-endings fluttering in anticipation. Unless she wanted to experience her first orgasm with this man by dry humping him all the way to the end, he needed to be inside her—now.

Massaging him from root to tip with one hand, Xiomara groped in her skirt pocket for the condom she'd stashed there before she'd left the hospital. 'Edmund,' she panted as she plucked it out, the galloping need to have him inside her becoming a fury in her brain.

'*Mmm?*' he murmured as he nuzzled his way up to her throat, his tongue swiping the shallow dip at the juncture of her collarbones.

'Condom,' she muttered, thrusting it at him.

Tearing his mouth from the side of her neck, Edmund obliged, his fingers apparently trembling as much as hers as he fumbled with the foil packet, cursing under his breath. 'Hell.' He gave a self-deprecating laugh. 'I'm shaking.'

Xiomara smiled, pleased at the note of disbelief in his voice, as if he wasn't used to being this kind of shook-up. She liked that he seemed out of his depth. 'Me too.'

Their gazes met then and despite the rapid-fire of her pulse and the erratic timbre of her breathing and the desperate signals from her body, they found a couple of beats of stillness for him to tear the packet open and toss it on the ground. Xiomara smiled triumphantly as he brandished the condom before reaching between their bodies and sheathing himself with stunning efficiency.

Sliding his hands to her hips then, he rucked up her long flowy skirt inch by inch, gathering the fabric at her sides as he went back to work on her neck, nuzzling her from the fast flutter of her carotid pulse to the angle of her jaw. Cool air, blissful on her heated skin, swirled around every inch of her exposed legs as more and more was slowly revealed, and when his fingers finally came into contact with the bare, dimpled flesh of her upper thigh he muttered, 'Yes,' in her ear.

Then, as his hands slid around to her butt, they stilled. Pulling away slightly, his gaze snared hers, a wicked smile spreading across his face. 'Princess, are you *commando* under there?'

Xiomara smiled. She'd removed her underwear in the bathroom, shoving it in her handbag at the same time she'd stashed the condom in her pocket. 'I thought it might be quicker.'

'Good thinking,' he muttered.

He kissed her then, hard and deep, and after

urging her to lock both legs around his waist, the blunt thickness of him notched at her entrance and then—blissfully, thankfully, surely—he thrust inside her with one flex of his hips, rocking her head against the wall and causing her to cry out and clutch at his shoulders.

'You okay?' he asked on a pant, his forehead pressed to her temple, puffs of his breathing disturbing the curls at her hairline.

Okay? Xiomara was better than okay. Her eyes shuttered at the influx of pleasure, stars popping behind her lids as the tight glove of her fluttered around him, precariously close to rippling out of control.

'Uh-huh,' she muttered, trying to catch the breath she'd lost to the mastery of his possession.

Xiomara had been with men before. And it had been fun and light and flirty. She'd had good lovers and rarely been disappointed in an experience but *this* was next level. She'd never been *had* like this. So totally and completely. As if he'd branded her with his mind as well as his body.

This was…*consummation.* And she hadn't even climaxed yet.

He groaned, deep and rumbly, his heated breath brushing her skin. 'You feel *good.*'

Xiomara gave a half laugh. *He* felt good. So good she was sure he'd have her there in one more thrust, which would be kinda embarrassing. Wasn't it supposed to be men who had issues with finishing too soon?

'I have to warn you,' she said as she prised her pleasure-heavy eyelids open. 'This isn't going to take long.'

He laughed, puffing more warm breath at her forehead. 'I've thought about doing this every waking and sleeping moment for the last four days. I won't be far behind you.'

And then he withdrew and entered again in one steady movement, causing Xiomara to cry out again and clutch him to her, one hand on his shoulder, the other buried in the hair at his nape, his chest smooshed against hers as he withdrew and thrust again.

And again.

And one more time as the flutters became ripples and the ripples became contractions, pulsing through her pelvic floor, shooting sparks up her spine and along every nerve-ending in her body. She cried out as the pleasure rocketed from zero to one hundred in a wave of pure bright incandescence.

'*Yes, yes, yes,*' he muttered, his breath hot at her neck, his big hands clutching the backs of her thighs, spreading her, angling her as he rocked himself in and out, the friction and motion pulling in all the right places. Every gasp from her dragged a corresponding groan from his throat as

94   FORBIDDEN FLING WITH THE PRINCESS

her walls clamped tight around him, their hearts slamming together in unison.

'*Dios*,' she moaned as everything started to break apart, the contractions taking over, engulfing her in light and sparks. '*Edmund*!'

She didn't know why she called his name with such desperation but she suddenly felt like she was falling and he was the only one who could catch her. The only one she wanted to catch her. And he did, he had her safe in his big hands, anchoring her to the wall, anchoring her to him.

'It's okay, I got you. I got you. Let go, *Xio*. Let it all out.'

Until that moment, Xiomara hadn't realised she had been holding it in. But his sexy, urgent rumblings had flipped some kind of switch undoing all that reserve and aloofness she'd needed to navigate royal life every second of the day. Every last pretention and hangup slipped away as she gave in to the pleasure rolling through her in deep, clenching waves. All of her ingrained reserve and polite formality dissolving as she gave herself up to the moment, letting the princess façade slip, crying out at the pleasure seeping into every cell in her body.

Something she'd never done before, some part of her always aware of the role she was playing. She'd worn her royal skin like a cloak, even being intimate with a man. Because that was what they expected. They wanted the princess.

But not this man. Edmund Butler didn't give a

damn about her royal pedigree. She could be herself. She could be *Xio*. She could just be a woman.

'Edmund,' she said again, deep and low on a long exhaled moan, revelling in the hedonism of her complete surrender.

'Xio...' he said, his shoulders quaking, his quads shaking as he thrust and thrust. 'God... *Xio*...you feel...so good.' A strangled kind of noise, somewhere between a gasp and a groan, spilled from his throat as his hips jerked to an abrupt halt for several long beats before he cried out in release.

Xiomara's pulse tripped at the guttural sound, so rich and unbridled as his thrusts resumed, disjointed and jerky. '*Yes,*' she moaned, turning her head and capturing his mouth. 'Yes, yes,' she said against his lips, licking in to him, kissing him deep and wet, swallowing his pleasure as he let go and lost himself inside her and she coasted through the misty remnants of her own pleasure.

Coasting and coasting until he was spent and so was she, but he was holding her there still, pinned by his big, hot, trembling body to the wall as if he couldn't move. Or didn't want to.

She certainly couldn't. And didn't. She never wanted to leave this spot.

She just wanted to wallow in the weight of his chest and the span of his shoulders and the hard bang of his heart shaking his ribcage—and hers.

Eventually, when the hot, husky raggedness of his breathing had settled and Xiomara didn't feel

96   FORBIDDEN FLING WITH THE PRINCESS

like her heart was going to explode, he stirred, pulling his head from the crook of her neck. His eyes roved over her face, which must look an absolute fright, her hair tossed about, her red lipstick completely kissed off.

'Now can I take you to a bed?' he asked, his voice gravelly, humour lighting his slumbrous amber gaze as it settled on hers.

Xiomara grinned. 'I think you're going to have to. I don't think I'll be able to walk.'

'Good.' He kissed her, brief and hard. 'Hold on.'

Not bothering to disentangle himself, he strode with her still attached to his person as if she weighed nothing, his big hands spanning the crease where her thighs met her ass and holding on tight. Xiomara clung to him, clutching the solid block of his shoulders, clamping her thighs tight around his hips, not wanting to break their intimate connection.

'I'm impressed you can carry me like this,' she admitted as he strode through a doorway. Xiomara knew she was no lightweight.

'You should be more impressed I'm actually capable of standing after that orgasm.'

She laughed. 'I'm impressed with that, too.'

He kissed her as he lowered her to his mattress in a flurry of skirts. 'Let me clean up,' he whispered, dropping a kiss on her nose. 'Don't go anywhere.'

Considering her legs still felt as weak and useless as wet noodles, Xiomara wasn't any kind of flight risk. She shivered as he withdrew then watched idly, too blissed-out to move as he headed for what she assumed was the en suite bathroom. From this angle, he appeared to be fully dressed although she knew he'd look less so from the front.

Still, she doubted he'd look as dishevelled as she was, spread on the bed, her bra cups pulled down, her skirt rucked up, her hair a springy tousled mess. She was utterly wrecked. Very different from the put-together princess image she always tried so hard to project.

The toilet flushed and, vaguely, Xiomara thought she should put herself to rights but her eyes drifted shut. Dopamine had her in its grip and she was happy to float along in the slipstream.

'God, you look beautiful.'

Xiomara smiled as her eyes drifted open. She was absolutely sure she did not—ravished maybe, not beautiful. But she could feel his eyes brushing over her body, lingering on her nipples, which hardened wantonly, and the note of absolute appreciation in his voice had her forgetting about her own inner critic.

Levering herself up, the flats of her forearms bent behind to support her, she opened her mouth to tell him flattery would get him *everywhere,* but the words lodged in her throat. He was naked, wearing nothing but a smile as he lounged in the en suite doorway, and there was no power on earth

98   FORBIDDEN FLING WITH THE PRINCESS

that could have stopped Xiomara's eyes from taking the tour.

Dark hair on his arms and legs and a light smattering on his chest emphasized his masculinity and Xiomara was helpless not to follow the line of hair that narrowed as it travelled down his abs, arrowing south until it became a thin trail from his belly button, bisecting the V of muscle between his hips, feathering out again as it got lost in the thatch of hair between his legs.

With the condom gone she could see *all* of him, his size big enough to widen her eyes as she inspected the part of his anatomy that had possessed her so thoroughly, hitting her in all the right places. Even in the aftermath he was impressively hung and butterflies fluttered in her belly as she thought about how good he might taste. What he might do if she rose from the bed right now, sank down on her knees before him and took him in her mouth.

His smile disappeared as his amber eyes heated to tawny. '*Xio*, I don't know what you're thinking right now—' He pushed off the doorway and prowled slowly in her direction. 'But your nipples just went hard as pennies.'

He was right—they had. Shamelessly sitting up and begging for more, almost painful in their tightness. Without thinking about it, she pressed the flats of her palms to them, trying to ease the tingle of arousal.

How could she want him again so soon? Wasn't

she completely spent five minutes ago? And yet desire stirred in her belly again.

'If you think that's helping,' he said with that amused tone in his voice she was coming to know so well, 'you're wrong.'

Their gazes met and held as he loomed over her now and suddenly the press of her palms was more erotic than soothing and the urge to arch her back rode her like the devil. Her breath tumbled from her lungs as she slowly squeezed her breasts, the hitch in his breath enormously gratifying.

'Tease,' he muttered, his gaze moving from her eyes to the play of her hands as she replaced her palms with her fingertips, brushing them across the erect tips of her nipples.

Xiomara smiled as her own gaze drifted, focusing on the thickening between his legs. 'Why are you all the way up there?' she asked.

'I have no idea,' he muttered as he planted a knee beside her and lowered himself down.

CHAPTER SIX

EDMUND STIRRED RELUCTANTLY the next morning, wrapped around Xiomara. Her warm back and bottom were snuggled into his front, his legs cocooned hers and his face was buried in her lush mop of curly hair. She smelled like jasmine and vanilla and something much earthier that spoke of their fevered sexual antics and he wondered why he was awake at five-thirty when he hadn't gone to sleep until after three.

Sure, his raging morning wood—not helped by the press of lush ass cheeks—was one reason, the early summer light poking in around the edge of the fancy blinds was another. Then he remembered the third.

The ultrasound.

He groaned internally. The last thing he wanted was to get out of this warm bed and leave this warm woman he was nowhere near finished with yet. But Phoebe and Octavio were giving the Institute one million pounds and for that they got extra special service. He might not know Phoebe very well but he knew women in this situation and, queen or not, she'd probably already be awake, counting down the minutes until he arrived.

He'd promised to be there at six and he wouldn't let them down just because he couldn't control his libido for a couple of hours.

Inhaling a clean hit of jasmine and vanilla, he gently tried to ease his arm out from under her neck. Xiomara had also had a late night and there was no point in them both being awake. He could make it to the hospital and back again within an hour and just slide in behind and wake her in a much more pleasant way.

'Mmm.' She grabbed his arm as he tried to extract it. 'Good morning.'

Edmund smiled at the drowsy satiation making her voice husky and enhancing her accent as he dropped kisses across her shoulder blade. So much for not waking her up.

'Go back to sleep,' he whispered. 'I'll be back in an hour. How do you like your coffee?'

Her hand slipped up and behind, anchoring around his neck, the sheet slipping down, giving Ed full access to her breasts—an invitation he wasn't about to ignore. He might have to be up and away very soon but he could linger for a little longer. He brushed a thumb across the brown tip, pulling a moan from her throat as she arched into his hand, the action thrusting her ass cheeks against his erection.

It took all his willpower not to *grind* as he played some more, urging her nipple into a hard peak. 'Edmund...' she said, barely audible as she

102   FORBIDDEN FLING WITH THE PRINCESS

rubbed the cleft of her ass against the aching hardness of his shaft.

Shutting his eyes to quell the sudden hot rush of desire, Ed kissed her neck and removed his hand. 'Later,' he whispered. 'Hold that thought.'

She protested sleepily as Ed reluctantly dragged himself from the bed, looking over his shoulder at the soft golden hue of her skin exposed from her shoulder to the cleft of her buttocks, the long stretch of her spine a tantalizing trail between. He wanted nothing more right now than to kiss his way up—or down—that golden road and it took all his willpower to turn away and leave the bed.

A quick *cold* shower helped dampen his ardour and ten minutes later he was dressed casually in ochre chinos and an untucked polo shirt with the Institute logo stitched over his left pectoral. It wasn't his usual work attire of business shirt, trousers and tie but he *was* still officially on vacation.

Finding both his bed and the room empty, he called, 'Xio?' as he made his way out.

Pulling up short in the doorway, he spied her on the far side of the open-plan living room, bending over to retrieve her handbag from the floor, where he did not recall it being dropped. From this vantage point he was able to see the rounded outline of her ass pressing against the fabric of the skirt as it fell forward and he looked his fill as he idly wondered if she was still commando underneath all those layers.

So much for that cold shower.

'Looks like I arrived at the right time,' he said.

Righting herself, she shot him a rueful smile as she turned to face him, her curls settling around her head as she slid her handbag over her shoulder. 'Why, Dr Butler—' she tutted as she gave him one of those *regal* looks she'd so perfected '—were you checking out my bottom?'

Ed grinned at how *proper* she made ass sound, even knowing it was deliberate. 'One hundred percent.'

'That's exceptionally uncouth of you.'

'I know, right?'

She laughed and it was light and tinkly and it made Ed grin even more as he shoved his hands in his pockets and just looked at her, his morning-after princess, her metaphoric tiara a little tainted after last night.

When her laughter settled, she asked, 'Can I catch a lift into the hospital with you?'

Oh. *Damn.* Ed had been hoping she'd be here when he got back but he supposed, given she'd been by Phoebe's side through everything, that she'd want to be there for the ultrasound too.

'You don't have to call your bodyguards?'

She smiled. 'Technically. But—' she shrugged '—I don't always do what I'm told.'

Edmund chuckled as he leaned into the door-frame. *Amen to that.* She certainly wasn't the put-together compliant princess he'd witnessed on

Castilona or the attentive royal courtier from the hospital yesterday. She looked like a woman who did as she pleased. She looked loose and messy and sated. She looked like she'd been well and truly ravaged.

And his heart kicked in his chest, knowing he'd been the one responsible.

'Umm, don't you think it'll be suspicious us arriving together?'

'No.' She frowned. 'I knew you were going to do the ultrasound at six and Phoebe wants me there for it. They'll just think we've run into each other on the way to the room.'

Ed laughed out loud. 'Xio. You're in the same clothes. I've known you for five days and never seen you in the same set of clothes. They'll know.'

She shrugged. 'They're pretty distracted right now.'

'Sure,' he conceded. 'But I still think one look at that thoroughly kissed mouth of yours will have Phoebe's female intuition pinging wildly.'

Smiling, she advanced towards him, slinking right into his space, her body pressed intimately against his, and Ed's breath hitched. He slid a hand onto her ass, holding her to him as a fresh surge of desire washed through his system. Her gaze fixed on his mouth as she raised a hand to it and trailed her index finger along first his bottom, then his top lip.

'The same could be said for yours.'

His lips tingled in response and Ed couldn't help himself, he opened his mouth and sucked her finger inside. The flare of her nostrils, the glow of those golden flecks in her eyes sent an electric charge through every last cell he owned.

She slid her finger from his mouth, trailing it down his throat as they stared at each other for long moments, the air pulsing with that charge now a tangible force between them.

'Right,' Ed said, clearing his throat as he brought himself back from the edge. 'My point exactly. They'll probably put two and two together. Distracted or not, they seem pretty smart.'

Her hand dropped away. 'Do you…' her brow crinkled '…not want them to know?'

Ed blinked as a subtle kind of tension permeated her frame. What? *No.* That was *not* what he'd meant. 'No.' He shook his head, his eyes locking on hers. 'Not at all,' he assured her. 'I just… didn't think *you'd* want them to. I assumed you kept things like this clandestine?'

Her body oozed against him as her tension eased. 'It's a bit hard having a clandestine anything when my security detail knows where I am and that I planned to stay the night.'

Okay, that *was* a good point.

'I suppose so.' He frowned. 'Don't you find that weird? That two people other than us know exactly what we were doing last night?'

He couldn't imagine a life where some third

106   FORBIDDEN FLING WITH THE PRINCESS

party was privy to what was essentially private information. To know his every movement. To know what he was doing behind closed doors.

'Oh, it's very weird.' She smiled but there was a resignation to it that put an itch up Ed's spine. 'But… I'm used to it. And their discretion is absolute.'

'So, they don't have to report your movements to the King?'

Her face scrunched into a horrified mask. 'Absolutely not.' She shuddered. 'I may be born into a royal family but I am an adult woman. Their job is to protect me, not to inform on me. The only time they would share details about my movements would be if something happened to me.'

Ed quirked a brow at that titbit. 'What do you mean? *Happened* to you?'

'Like an attack or an abduction.'

She said it so casually. Attack. Abduction. As if the threat of violence was just another part of her life. It made him want to wrap her up and never let her out of his sight. It made him grateful for her protection, as weird and unnatural and intrusive as it felt.

'Has that ever happened?'

'No.' She shook her head, her curls jostling at the movement. 'Mostly they protect me from photographers. The Castilona royal family is hardly well known, but there's a group of the paparazzi who make their living from snaps of young Euro-

AMY ANDREWS 107

pean royals. Although when I was younger, when my father was Regent, plans were uncovered for a kidnapping but—'

'*What?*' Ed gaped at her casual announcement.

She shrugged. 'They were early plans and the people were amateurs apparently.'

Ed shook his head, not quite able to absorb the enormity of a kidnap plot. It was the stuff of fiction and yet this was Xiomara's life. 'How do you live like that?'

She smiled and raised herself on her tippy-toes. 'One day at a time,' she murmured against his mouth then kissed him lightly. 'Now—' she dropped back onto the soles of her feet, her hands sliding to sit flat against his pecs '—don't we have to get to the hospital?'

Clearly, she was done talking about the strictures of her life but Ed couldn't help being a little freaked out. 'Are you sure we shouldn't call your bodyguards? You were followed by the paparazzi yesterday, remember?'

She'd told him about their James Bond drive to his apartment in bed last night and they'd laughed at the anecdote. But in the cold light of day, with the knowledge of much more sinister happenings, it wasn't so funny.

'Positive.' She nodded with absolute certainty. 'We gave them the slip. Nobody knows I'm here.'

'How can you be sure?'

'Because they'd have probably already found a

ladder or hired a crane or something to get a picture through your windows.'

Ed shuddered. 'That's terrible.'

'Yes. It is.'

Her acceptance of the bizarreness of it all was probably the most grounding thing of all and ordinarily he'd just dismiss it with a *rather you than me* quip. But Xiomara wasn't some tabloid princess from a faraway land any more. She was flesh and blood. She'd been in his bed. He'd kissed *every* inch of her body. He'd been *inside* her.

She was real. And he *liked* her. A lot.

'It's okay,' she whispered conspiratorially, a smile playing on her mouth where she'd dashed some of that demure, princess-pink gloss. 'It doesn't happen that often. Now—' she took a step away and held out her hand '—we should go or we're going to be late.'

He smiled and took her hand but all Ed really wanted to do was throw her over his shoulder and take her back to his bed and give her some kind of reprieve from *that* kind of life. Offer her shelter in *his* life.

And hell if that wasn't new.

No woman had ever made him contemplate making room for anything other than his work— he had one ex-fiancée to prove it. Ed supposed that should be a cause for alarm.

Strangely, it wasn't.

* * *

At this hour of morning the two-mile drive was barely affected by traffic and Ed turned into the doctors' car park twelve minutes after pulling out of the basement parking garage at his Kensington apartment. There were only a few other cars there as he drove into his dedicated parking space, shaded by the vibrant summer foliage of one of the many plane trees that bordered the parking area.

There was no sign of any paparazzi on the street across the road from the hospital entrance as there had been when he'd left yesterday. Hospital security had moved the clutch of photographers off the grounds but hadn't been able to do anything about them setting up camp on the opposite side of the street.

Clearly, though, they'd got what they came for. That, or it was just too early for them.

Ed offered Xiomara his hand as she had offered hers in the apartment and the fact she took it as easily as he had put a zing up his arm and a glow in his chest. He couldn't remember if a woman had ever had such a visceral, electrifying effect on his body.

Sure, he'd desired women before that he'd felt in physical ways. But not like this. Like a magnet vibrating with potential as the right pull entered its electrical field.

The sky was a soft gauzy mauve, promising to deepen and flourish into a decent summer's day,

110   FORBIDDEN FLING WITH THE PRINCESS

as they headed for the entrance. Her steps slowed, however, as they neared and she drew to a halt as she shot him a nervous smile. 'Please tell me this is all going to be fine. I feel bad that I've given this zero thought all night.'

Ed liked that he'd been the one responsible for keeping Xiomara preoccupied enough to forget about the twins for a while. She'd been intensely focused on them and finding a solution to their condition since it had been identified only days ago, which was incredibly selfless. But the correct procedure had been performed in an expert and timely manner so she'd deserved a break from the mental load of it all.

He smiled reassuringly. 'I have every confidence.' He locked his eyes on hers so she could *see* his confidence—lean into it. 'But if you're asking me for a one hundred percent assurance that the procedure was a success, I can't give you that.'

It was the truth. He couldn't. And it was important to acknowledge that sometimes things didn't go according to plan. Something he'd already discussed in great depth with Octavio and Phoebe.

'But I've done this hundreds of times, and complications have been *exceptionally* rare.'

The thing was, *he* knew *she* knew what they were because Xiomara's research had been thorough. And now they were faced with finding out, it was only natural those things would be on her mind. They were in the back of his mind as well, despite being extremely happy with how the procedure had gone.

'Okay.' She gave him a wobbly smile. 'Thank you.'

Ed returned the smile as he slid his hand to her face, cupping her cheek, his finger furrowing into her hair. 'Please tell *me* your cousin and his wife know how lucky they are to have such an amazing advocate.'

'It has been mentioned,' she murmured, a smile curving her mouth as his lips lowered towards her.

He kissed her then, in the middle of the deserted car park, because it seemed like an age since he'd kissed her in the apartment and he was swept up in her heart and her empathy and well... he couldn't *not*. He couldn't, it seemed, get enough of her mouth.

'Okay now?' he asked as he pulled away.

She nodded. 'Okay now.'

Sliding his arm around her shoulders, he said, 'Let's go look at some royal babies.'

First, though, they had to run the gauntlet of royal security.

There was a different guy in black stationed outside the door with Xavier this morning. 'Your Royal Highness,' different guy greeted, his accent thick. 'You were supposed to call us to come pick you up.'

Xiomara smiled prettily. 'I know.'

Ed blinked as Xiomara morphed into the prin-

112 FORBIDDEN FLING WITH THE PRINCESS

cess before his eyes. All demure and charming, like butter wouldn't melt in her mouth. Like she hadn't ridden him like a cowgirl last night. He wondered how often she used that façade to get out of trouble.

Or get her way.

'I'm so sorry, Felipe,' she continued. 'But Edmund was coming here anyway. It seemed pointless and such an imposition, not to mention entirely environmentally unfriendly to have two cars out on the road.'

Felipe's expression remained impassive. 'It is never an imposition, Princess.'

'Never,' Xavier reiterated as his gaze settled on Ed.

There was no outward sign that he was hacked off, but Ed could feel the disapproval coming off him in waves. Not that he could blame the guy. It was his job to protect Xiomara and, given what he knew now, Ed was grateful that there were trained people who had her back. 'We take Her Royal Highness's protection very seriously, *sir*. We'd appreciate your cooperation so we can do our jobs and ensure her safety at all times.'

In his peripheral vision, Ed could see Xiomara's lips pressed together, clearly amused at the achingly polite dressing-down by her bodyguard. He ignored her but absolutely planned on making her pay a little bit when he got her alone later.

Ed inclined his head in acknowledgement of

Xavier's more than reasonable security request. 'Absolutely. You have it.'

'Apologies again, Xavier,' Xiomara said, shooting him another one of her pretty smiles before turning to Ed. 'Shall we?'

She didn't wait for his answer, just sailed past all three men as she headed for the door of the hospital suite as if she was walking a rope line somewhere and not all sexily dishevelled from rolling around in his bed. And hell if that wasn't a very inconvenient turn-on.

Ed was right about Phoebe counting down the minutes until he arrived. He entered the room about a minute after Xiomara, pushing the hefty piece of ultrasound equipment he'd arranged to be left outside the room. Phoebe greeted him with a huge smile that did little to hide both the flood of relief and the anxiety underpinning it all.

'Good morning,' he said as he smiled at her and Octavio.

They returned his greeting but neither of them looked particularly well rested.

'Good morning, Dr Butler,' Xiomara murmured in her cool princess voice with her best *resting royal face* firmly in place as he manoeuvred the machine to her side of the bed.

The closer he got, though, the clearer he could see the daring imp dancing in her gaze. She was obviously enjoying the clandestine flirting and

114   FORBIDDEN FLING WITH THE PRINCESS

the undercurrent flowing like a river of lava between them.

'Morning,' he said with a nod, all cool professional despite the *I'm-going-to-get-you-for-that-you-little-minx* look he shot her as she moved out of his way, rounding to the other side of the bed, taking up position next to her cousin.

Getting his head back in the game, Ed made all the usual enquiries of Phoebe as he fired up the machine. How did she sleep? Had the epidural completely worn off? Had she eaten and been to the toilet? Did she have any pain? Any contractions? Any discomfort? Any leakage of fluid? Any decrease in the foetal movements?

All the things the royal couple had been advised to watch for and call him should any occur.

As soon as the machine was ready, Ed got straight to it, knowing from their stilted replies that neither King nor Queen had the heart for small talk.

'There they are,' he said as he slid the transducer through the gel he'd squirted on Phoebe's bare belly.

A grainy flurry of arms and legs bobbling around in their watery world filled the screen and three sets of eyes homed in on the picture on his screen. There was no large wall-mounted TV in this suite so Ed angled the machine, giving everyone access to his screen.

Octavio kissed his wife's forehead as she said, 'How does it look?' her voice slightly tremulous.

'One moment, let me just—' Ed moved the transducer around a little until he got the view he was after—the donor twin's bladder. He smiled triumphantly. 'I see urine.'

'You do?' Phoebe said with a sniffle.

'That's it there?' Octavio asked, pointing at a black bubble that had not been on yesterday's ultrasound.

'Yes, that's it,' Ed confirmed with a grin, as relieved to see it as everyone else in the room if the collective release of breath was any indication.

He'd been confident in the way that being an expert in his field afforded him, but he also knew that very occasionally the procedure wasn't successful or a rare complication might arise so it was always good to have this confirmation.

'And I can see there's already been an increase in the donor amniotic fluid,' Ed added as he returned his attention to the screen, pushing some buttons to accurately calculate the volume for comparison.

'Oh, thank God,' Phoebe muttered, pressing one hand to her chest as her husband kissed the other and held it close. 'I've been trying to stay positive but it's hard not to worry.'

'Of course,' Ed assured her. 'That's only natural.'

His gaze slid to Xiomara, who was smiling at

116   FORBIDDEN FLING WITH THE PRINCESS

him not with relief or gratitude, but with *pride* shining from her eyes. 'See,' she said as she looked at him lingeringly before switching her attention to Phoebe. 'Didn't I tell you two he was the best?'

Phoebe laughed. 'You did. He's a miracle worker.'

Octavio turned relieved eyes on him. 'You just might be. I don't think I will ever be able to thank you enough for what you've achieved here.'

Ed shrugged off the compliment. Yes, what he did was highly specialised and he *was* the best in his field but, at its core, it was a simple enough procedure. It wasn't complex like open-heart surgery or complicated like putting a smashed bone back together or convoluted like organ transplantation.

He wasn't superhuman. Or a superhero. Or a miracle worker.

And because Xiomara wasn't looking at him like he was any of those things but looking at him like he was first and foremost a *man* and with *pride* instead of relief and gratitude it meant more than the King's praise.

'Okay.' Ed moved the transducer to get a look at the recipient twin. 'Let's just do some more checks while we're here.'

Fifteen minutes later, he was wiping goop off the royal belly, chatting with two very different people, loose and laughing and relaxed now.

'You can leave as soon as you're ready today to go back to the consulate,' he said. 'But please take it easy for these next few days. You are at a higher risk of pre-term labour and membrane complications due to the procedure.'

Ed had already been through the risks associated with the surgery—both during and after—but he repeated them again because he understood that parents weren't often in a state to absorb information about post-op management when they hadn't yet been through the procedure. Their focus was understandably on the more immediate issue.

'I will make sure of that,' Octavio confirmed in a gruff voice, giving his wife an uncompromising look. Not that she seemed inclined to argue. This pregnancy complication had obviously shaken her.

'If you'd like to come in tomorrow for another ultrasound? Maybe—' he slid a quick glance at Xiomara '—not quite so early?'

Phoebe laughed then apologised. 'Absolutely. So sorry about getting you out at the crack of dawn. What time would suit you? You name it—' she smiled at Octavio '—we'll be here.'

'How about…' Another quick look Xiomara's way was executed without being noticed and Ed was thankful that the royal couple seemed too caught up in their relief and jubilation to notice the undercurrent between him and Xiomara.

She mouthed, '*Nine.*'

Nine sounded perfectly respectable.

'How about nine? I dare say you could use the sleep-in,' he said, knowing full well the King and

118   FORBIDDEN FLING WITH THE PRINCESS

Queen of Castilona weren't the only ones in the room who could use the extra sleep.

A certain princess could, too. He wouldn't say no either. Or they could wake early and have amazing morning sex, all sleepy and tender, and not have to tumble straight from bed to the hospital.

'Perfect,' Phoebe agreed.

'What time shall I order the car for?' Xiomara asked Octavio as she pulled her phone out of her bag. Not waiting for his reply, she turned to Phoebe. 'And would you like some of those ahmazing little pastries from Harrods you love so much?' Her thumbs flew over the keys. 'I don't think it'll be too late to get them delivered for morning tea.'

'Xiomara—' Phoebe laughed, stilling the rapid-fire tapping of her fingers '—it's fine. You don't have to do any of that. You've gone above and beyond for us but Octavio is perfectly capable of taking care of me. Why don't you ring some of your friends? Go out on the town? It's London. You *love* London. Go have some fun.'

Ed tensed at the thought of her *having fun* out there in his city that didn't involve him. Yeah, that wasn't going to happen. If she wanted to go out, *he'd* take her. But he needn't have worried. One look at Xiomara's dumbstruck expression told him not only that she hadn't been expecting the directive but the idea didn't appeal.

'Oh.' She blinked then waved her hand dismissively. 'I'm having fun.'

Her gaze slid his way and a frisson passed between them that lifted the hairs on his nape. It was so palpable, Ed felt sure the other two occupants of the room must also be able to feel it, but it appeared not. Phoebe did, however, intercept *the look,* her eyes suddenly narrowing as they moved back and forth from Ed to Xiomara and back to Ed.

Just as he had suspected, once the cause of Phoebe's preoccupation was resolved she'd likely not miss much, so he tried really hard to *not* look like he'd spent all night debauching the Princess of Castilona. But the more he tried to empty his mind, the more unhelpful images it delivered.

Phoebe frowned at Xiomara. 'Isn't that the same outfit you were wearing yesterday?'

'Oh.' Xiomara glanced down at her clothes. 'These? Yeah… I'd slung them over the chair next to the bed last night and then I overslept my alarm this morning so I just grabbed them and threw them on.' She shrugged as if it was no big deal. 'I'll change when we get back to Belgravia.'

Phoebe's gaze met Octavio's, and he raised an eyebrow as if he didn't quite know where this was going but that something was definitely hinky with his usually put-together cousin. Returning her attention to Ed, Phoebe continued her friendly interrogation. 'And your plans for the day?' But before he could answer she said, 'More… Netflix?'

120   FORBIDDEN FLING WITH THE PRINCESS

Ed wasn't sure how to play this. He was thirty-four-years-old, not some spotty teenager who needed to account for his every move to his girlfriend's suspicious friends.

But then he'd never slept with a princess before.

Phoebe got in again before he answered. 'Or maybe a little—' another look at Xiomara, and a very definite twitch of her lips as if she was having a little fun now '—chill?'

Octavio narrowed his eyes as Phoebe looked pointedly at Xiomara. Ed recognized the minute the penny dropped for the King, a slow smile lighting his face.

'Maybe,' he lied, still hedging even though he knew for damn sure there was going to be a lot of *chill* going on today.

'Hmm.' Phoebe crossed her arms and stared at a fixed point in the air for a few beats as if contemplating something, before returning her attention to him. 'You know who loves TV?'

Octavio, getting in on the matchmaking action, chimed in. 'Xiomara does.'

Ed couldn't help but smile as he finally glanced at Xiomara. 'I mean…' he shrugged '…if the Princess wanted to join me…'

Xiomara grinned. 'The Princess would.'

It was somehow old-fashioned to be having this deliberately roundabout conversation and yet that was part of its appeal. Ed felt as if he'd been given some kind of royal stamp of approval. Not that he needed one—he and Xiomara were both adults and this was just *chill* after all—but it was surprisingly nice to have.

And he was far too old to be sneaking around. Xiomara's security considerations were more than enough cloak-and-dagger for him.

More than enough.

CHAPTER SEVEN

XIOMARA LINGERED THE following morning after
Tavi and Phoebe had left Edmund's rooms, where
the second ultrasound had taken place. They'd both
been practically walking on air as the results confirmed that the TTTS was slowly improving. Edmund had been quick to reiterate that it usually
took two weeks for the condition to completely
resolve but he was clearly pleased that things were
heading in the right direction.

As were Tavi and Phoebe.

Xavier was waiting outside to accompany her to
the car. She was following the royal couple back
to the consulate for a few hours to play hostess for
Tavi as he welcomed a dignitary from the European parliament who'd requested an urgent meeting regarding agricultural subsidies whilst he was
in London.

Unfortunately, wherever in the world Tavi travelled, his job always travelled with him. And no
matter what was going on in his personal life, the
people of Castilona expected their King to attend
to matters of state. That was just the way it was
and it wasn't something, as members of the royal
family, they ever really questioned. Dedication to

subjects and country was not only a birthright but a privilege.

On top of that, Xiomara knew that Tavi felt he had to be especially accessible and steadfast in these early days after the mercurial whims of her father's reign.

Since their marriage, Phoebe had done the hostess duties but Tavi had insisted she rest and that he could handle it himself. And, of course, he could. He was a superb leader and diplomat for their kingdom. But Xiomara knew the role upside down and inside out. It was what she'd been *born* to do and, as such, could converse on a wide range of topics from the frivolous right through to more serious matters of state with the intuition to know which was required when.

So, she didn't mind stepping in for Phoebe. As with Tavi, her duty to Castilona was paramount.

But she'd also be counting down the minutes until she could be back in Edmund's bed. The last two nights had been magical in a way she'd never had before. Her lips curved thinking about them. And it wasn't about the sex. Or not *just* the sex anyway because that had been spectacular. It had been how anonymous she'd felt.

How she could just be herself.

Like any other woman in the first flush of a giddy sexual fling, when the only thing on her mind was the next encounter. Not whether the person she was with was going to sell the details to a gossip blog. Or whether he was genuinely interested in her for her or for her royal pedigree and royal bank account. Or whether he expected her to be a princess between the sheets.

Which meant she stuck to a particular circle of people. *Who all knew each other.* No anonymity there. She'd always been Princess Xiomara with any other guy. But not in Edmund's apartment. Not in his bed. Not in his arms. She wasn't a princess when she was with him.

She was a *woman.* And that was exhilarating.

She just wished they could have that outside his apartment, too. Being in bed twenty-four-seven was no hardship but, as Phoebe had said, Xiomara loved London and she'd love nothing more than to step out into it with Edmund at her side. This was his hometown after all—how amazing would it be to see it through his eyes?

How amazing would it be to just be able to walk outside the apartment with him, go for a stroll, get some fresh air? Laze in Hyde Park with all the other people watching the row boats on the Serpentine. Jump in a glass bubble for a spin around the Eye. Wander through Borough Market. If they'd been in Castilona together, she'd have taken him all over.

But London was a whole other ball game security-wise.

Except maybe if they got out of the capital. Away from the gaggle of paparazzi on the hospital *and* consulate doorsteps. The next ultrasound wasn't for five days…and as long as they didn't go too far in case of complications, why not? Her lips curved into a smile at the thought of being anonymous *outside* his apartment. Wandering around like lovers in the English countryside without a single person knowing who she was.

'I know what you're thinking.'

Two big arms slid around her waist from behind as Edmund nuzzled her temple and Xiomara's smile grew. Turning in his arms, her breath caught in her throat. She kept forgetting how classically good-looking he was and how his whiskery scruff enhanced his sexiness. But it was the *way* he looked at her that truly robbed her of her ability to breathe.

Not because he knew who she was, but because he liked what he saw.

Xiomara locked her green gaze with his amber one. 'You want to get out of here?'

He laughed. 'Sure. But don't you have that thing you have to do?'

'I mean after. Let's get out of the city. Somewhere away from the capital. A quaint little village, or a pebbly beach. Within an easy drive of London, of course, but away from it all. There's five days until the next ultrasound and your holiday *did* get interrupted.'

'Like…camping?'

He was teasing but she didn't care. She'd rough-it for him. She'd lie down under any roof with this man—even a canvas one. 'Anywhere.'

He didn't immediately jump in and proclaim it a fabulous idea and a sense that she'd got things wildly wrong filled the silence. She'd been so swept up in the abandon of the last two nights she'd thought that meant he'd want to spend the rest of her time in London together.

She winced internally. Rookie move, *Princess*. This was sex. They weren't dating.

'Oh God, I'm sorry,' she apologised, feeling like an idiot. 'That was very presumptuous of me. Forget I said anything.' Xiomara pushed against his chest to be released, mortified.

But Edmund's arms only tightened, 'Hey. No.' He slid a hand onto her cheek as he captured her gaze. 'Xio.' He smiled softly before dropping a string of soft kisses on her mouth that soothed and stirred in equal measure. 'Not presumptuous. Not even a little. I think it's a wonderful idea.'

Another kiss this time and Xiomara leaned into it as it deepened, relief and the low rumble of his groan igniting the embers of passion. Her heart was racing when he eventually dragged his mouth from hers.

'My only concern,' he said, his forehead pressed to hers, his breath fanning her face, 'is your security detail. It's hardly a romantic mini-break when there's two guys in black shadowing us everywhere.'

AMY ANDREWS 127

The R word did little to calm Xiomara's pulse. She hadn't thought of it as a *romantic mini-break* but she loved the sound of it. It seemed so terribly English. Something regular, normal, ordinary English *couples* did.

And she wanted that with him so very much.

Xiomara pulled away a little so she could look into his eyes. 'Trust me, they can be a lot more discreet than that.'

But he had a point.

Xiomara trusted Xavier with her life—literally. He was efficient and strategic but also flexible, aware that things often changed at a moment's notice, so he had contingencies for everything. Pretty much the way his mother had once run the royal kitchens! But, more than that, she'd got to know him personally after several years of travelling together and she liked him. Hell, theirs was probably the longest relationship she'd ever had with a man.

But she didn't want him along for *this* ride.

'I can ask Tavi to have it withdrawn. He won't be a fan, neither will Xavier, but Phoebe is definitely team *Ed*.' She smiled at him. 'So, I think he could be convinced.'

Edmund chuckled and it was deep and warm and rich and Xiomara wanted to curl up and purr. 'Yes, but…' his brow crinkled '…*should* you?'

Xiomara had been aware when she'd shared the information about her near kidnapping as a child that it had disturbed Edmund, but she hadn't re-

128   FORBIDDEN FLING WITH THE PRINCESS

alised quite how much. She tended to forget that security guards with guns weren't *normal*.

'There's no current credible threat to me as far as I'm aware so it's really only paparazzi we have to worry about. I doubt Tavi would consider my request if we were staying in London. Not with the paps knowing the de la Rosas are in town and especially not after the statement concerning the health of the royal babies goes out this afternoon. There'll be a bit of a flurry to get first pics.'

She rolled her eyes. Sometimes even she couldn't believe her own life.

'But if we can give them the slip, which is generally easy enough, and stay away from major centres, it should be fine. Xavier will put a bunch of contingencies in place in case things go pearshaped but I've done it before when I've been away with friends. I'm not that well known here, not like one of your royal family.'

'What does *not that well known* mean? Exactly how recognizable are you?'

She quirked an eyebrow. '*You* didn't recognize me.'

He chuckled. 'Yes, but I'm hardly in that demographic, am I?'

'I doubt I'm recognizable at all here unless you're a pap or someone who's really into the royal-watching scene. If I wear my hair back and some sunglasses when I'm out and about, my own cousin would probably walk straight past me.'

AMY ANDREWS   129

'So…don't pack your tiara?'

Xiomara laughed. She loved how casual…how flippant he was about her pedigree. As if being a royal princess was the least interesting thing about her. Most non-aristocratic men she'd dated would have already peppered her with questions about who she did and didn't know in those circles. But not Edmund. He'd never once asked her if she knew Meghan or Harry.

'Exactly.'

'All right. Let's do it.' He smiled then and it was slow and lazy and promised all kinds of wicked things that made her insides loop-the-loop. 'A good friend of mine has a small holiday cottage in Cornwall. It's on a headland overlooking the sea and St Ives, and the weather for the remainder of this week is supposed to be sunny. I could find out if it's available?'

Xiomara's heart sang at the suggestion. 'It sounds great.'

In fact, it sounded perfect.

Just like him.

Six hours later, Xiomara was watching the sparkle of sun on the ocean as Edmund navigated the clifftop road. It might be almost five in the afternoon but the sun of high summer was still several hours off setting. She couldn't believe she was here and had to stop from pinching herself.

It hadn't taken long to get Tavi on board but,

130   FORBIDDEN FLING WITH THE PRINCESS

as expected, Xavier had been more hesitant. Still, ever the professional, once the King had approved it, he had set about ensuring that Xiomara could get away undetected and have some plans in place should she need to be extracted quickly.

And here they were, almost at the cottage Edmund had arranged.

Xiomara had felt guilty about leaving Phoebe, who was essentially confined to the consulate. They had become close friends over the past six months, and she was in London, in part, to be a companion, a lady-in-waiting figure for Phoebe when Tavi couldn't be around.

Phoebe, though, had been insistent that Xiomara leave. 'I'm a grown woman,' she'd said with a roll of her eyes. 'I don't need a *companion.*'

As the new Queen, Phoebe had settled well into royal life but Xiomara knew she found the strictures and traditions both surreal and jarring.

'You like him?' she'd asked.

'Yes.'

'*Like* him, like him? Or just, *I'm-in-town-for-a-week* like him?'

Xiomara had smiled. Phoebe was clearly thrilled to see Xiomara enjoying herself but it was just as clear she was worried about Xiomara potentially getting hurt when they headed back to Castilona and Edmund went to Africa. But Xiomara knew it could be nothing more than a pleasant interlude and had assured Phoebe of such.

The car slowed. 'Almost there,' Edmund said.

He turned off the main road onto a bumpy narrow lane, changing Xiomara's view to the nearby clutter and colour of St Ives at the bottom of the headland. The sun reflected off the strip of white sand and the windows of the houses and shopfronts that lined the area between the two piers. Fishing boats bobbed at anchor in the shallow harbour, the water a clear, tranquil aquamarine, the seaweed-encrusted mooring ropes on the sandy bottom clearly visible even at a distance.

'Tide's in,' Edmund said. 'When it goes out the entire harbour empties.'

Xiomara had never been to Cornwall before. In many ways it was similar to Castilona—old buildings, harbour, beaches. But that was where the similarities ended. The Mediterranean light was different—warm and golden, drenching the land beneath it in a heat that spoke of summer grape harvests and long, lazy siestas. Still, she was excited to explore this very English seaside setting, although she'd have been excited to explore anywhere with Edmund.

They passed several cottages strung along the lane before he pulled up outside a small whitewashed building with blue detailing around the door as well as several large windows that dominated the front aspect and on top of the low whitewashed wall that formed the front fence. There

132 FORBIDDEN FLING WITH THE PRINCESS

was nothing but fields behind them and a view of cliffs, ocean and town in front.

'Oh,' she said on a sigh. 'This is beautiful.'

He leaned across, slid a hand to her nape and kissed her and Xiomara melted into it, into him, her heart light as air in her chest. 'You're beautiful,' he muttered against her mouth, his voice deliciously husky as he pulled away, her red lipstick now almost completely kissed off. 'Come on, let's have a look around and then go into St Ives for some dinner. The seafood here is amazing.'

Xiomara exited the car, the sun warm on shoulders covered only by the shoestring straps of her floaty yellow sundress, a light breeze ruffling her curls. She slipped her hand into his as he rounded the vehicle and they walked through the little gate that led to a stone path that took them straight to the front door, which wasn't locked.

Edmund's friend had arranged for the cottage to be readied for them, including a supply of groceries to be delivered that were sitting in shopping bags on the island bench when they walked inside.

'This is perfect,' Xiomara said as she took in the very modern open-plan living, dining and kitchen area that had obviously been renovated to a very high spec.

Thick walls, half whitewashed, half exposed to reveal a glorious honey stone hinted at its age as well as adding character. Large weathered honey-brown flagstones formed the floor. The sea side was dominated by two large picture windows, one in the kitchen, where the sink was located to take full advantage of the view, the other in the living area, the natural wall thickness creating a cosy window seat and providing an unspoiled panorama of cliffs and ocean.

The other side of the living area was dominated by an inglenook fireplace that would no doubt keep the little cottage toasty when the winter evenings drew in and the sea turned squally.

'The bedroom is through here,' Edmund said.

It wasn't huge but with a large bed sporting plush bedding sitting against the wall opposite and another picture window looking out to sea, it was all they needed. On the wall behind the bed a doorway led to a roomy en suite bathroom with a walk-in shower *and* a clawfoot tub situated in front of yet another huge window that looked out over the fields beyond.

It was a stunning view. And the bath was big enough for two!

'It's not a palace,' Ed said as Xiomara stepped back in the bedroom. 'But I reckon it'll do for a few days.'

She quirked an eyebrow. 'Do you think I need a palace?' Sure, she *lived* in a palace and she was used to luxury, but that didn't mean she couldn't appreciate the charm and beauty and all the love and care that had obviously gone into renovating this cosy space.

134 FORBIDDEN FLING WITH THE PRINCESS

But mostly, she hated that he might think her so pampered that only luxury would do.

He shrugged. 'I…don't know? Do you?'

It was a fair question, she supposed, but it still stung. Sure, she'd landed in a helicopter and plucked him off a beach in the middle of the Indian Ocean, but she'd thought she'd proven to him at least the last two nights that she didn't need buglers and gold toilet seats wherever she went, and she didn't expect airs and graces.

'No.' Although what came to the tip of her tongue was *I just need you.*

Crossing to the hip-high window that extended almost to the ceiling, she stood and admired the vista, placing the flats of her palms on the deep ledge. She leaned close to the glass, her eyes tracking down the lane they'd taken, across the grassy expanse of the clifftop dotted with yellow and white wildflowers to where the town dipped towards the ocean. Edmund snuggled his body in behind hers and she sighed contentedly.

A remote control gadget sat in the corner and she reached for it. 'What's this for?'

Taking it from her hand, Edmund flicked the button, causing the entire window to frost over, cocooning them in a bubble of privacy.

'*Nice,*' Xiomara murmured in appreciation.

'Yep. Triple-glazed to reduce the noise from the howling winds and squalls that can batter this place. And electrochromic for complete privacy.

All the windows are the same. Thacks and Vi thought of everything.'

He flicked it again, the glass becoming transparent once more, the ocean and cliffs appearing as if by magic. Placing the remote down, his palms slid onto the ledge, caging her against the sill as his mouth brushed her temple.

'I never get tired of this view.'

His voice was rich with innuendo, leaving her in little doubt it wasn't the outside he was talking about as the heat of his gaze fixed on the rise of her breasts, outlined perfectly in the firm yet stretchy shirring of the bodice of the dress. But her smile faded as Xiomara wondered suddenly, did he actually mean something different?

'Have you been here before?'

He seemed to know a lot about it after all, and this was a cottage for *lovers*.

Had he brought some other woman here? Had he laid her on the bed behind them, rolled around with her, gone down on her? Had he stood at this very window and ground against her?

'Yes,' he murmured as he dropped kisses down the side of her neck.

'With a…woman?'

Xiomara hadn't meant for her voice to be quite so high on that last word but it obviously cut through Edmund's ardour as he stilled.

'Xio,' he murmured, his warm lips brushing her cheekbone. 'Are you jealous?'

136   FORBIDDEN FLING WITH THE PRINCESS

He sounded amused but his enquiry caused a mini riot inside her head. No. Yes. Oh, dear...*was she*? Or had his palace quip just made her hypersensitive?

Gah! This wasn't her. She *wasn't* hypersensitive and it was none of her business.

But she wasn't sure she could stay here if he had. Which was stupid, she knew. And possibly exceptionally spoiled of her. Just because she'd never been on a romantic mini-break before didn't mean he hadn't. Possibly right here. And, like a ghoulish spectator at a car crash, she couldn't look away.

She needed to know.

'Curious,' she said evasively. 'Have you?'

His arms circled her waist as he propped his chin on her head. 'I've been here twice,' he confirmed, his voice matter-of-fact. 'Once for a weekend, when a bunch of us helped with the internal painting when Thacks and Vi were renovating, though we all slept at an Airbnb in St Ives. The second time when they held a housewarming to celebrate it being done and it was the middle of a heatwave and we all camped under the stars in the field out the back.'

Xiomara shut her eyes on a wave of relief.

'Okay?' he murmured.

He didn't sound angry or impatient that she'd asked. He wasn't getting all moody and he hadn't walked away. She'd asked, he'd answered. Done.

She nodded. 'Okay.'

'Good. Now—' His hands slid to her breasts. 'Where were we?'

He squeezed them and a low moan rolled from her throat, a wave of heat cascading south from the tip of her nipples and intensifying as it crested straight between her thighs.

'You want to try out the bed?' he whispered as his mouth buzzed her ear.

'No.' Beyond the cliffs and the town the ocean was big and vast and wild and it drove something equally wild and reckless inside. 'Here.' She slid her hands over the top of his as he kneaded.

'Mmm,' he muttered. 'Get the window.'

'No,' she repeated, then yanked the shirring of her top down, her unfettered breasts spilling out, exposing them to full view of anyone who might be passing by.

Okay, the road was hardly a major thoroughfare, but the thought that somebody *could* be out walking on the cliffs was a wicked little thrill cranking her arousal. This was not something Princess Xiomara could ever contemplate doing, taking something so private and flaunting it in a very public way. There could be telephoto lenses trained on them.

Prying eyes.

But here on the rugged Cornish coast she was just Xio and he was just *Ed* and a feral kind of abandon coursed through her system.

'*Xio*,' he groaned, his hands cupping the lush

138 FORBIDDEN FLING WITH THE PRINCESS

spill of her, his fingers rolling her rapidly hardening nipples.

She cried out at the exquisite torment of it, pressing back into him as she lifted her arms and circled them around his neck, thrusting her breasts into his palms.

'You want this here?' he muttered into her hair, his voice thick with arousal as he rubbed his thumbs over nipples that were now tingling with an urgent need that could well drive her out of her mind. 'In full view of the window?'

'Yes,' she panted. *One hundred times, yes.*

'There's a car coming.'

There was no hitch in his voice, no alarm or concern that they were going to be caught in flagrante delicto. It was more a low, lazy hum as he pinched the peaked tips of her breasts, shooting an entire quiverful of flaming arrows straight to her clit, lighting up the pleasure centre of her brain. She cried out at the pure delicious twist of it, arching her back, thrusting her chest, rolling her hips in pure hedonistic pleasure.

Xiomara vaguely saw the flash of sunlight on paintwork as the car made its way ever closer along the pockmarked road but she was so tuned in to the magic of Ed's touch and her baser desires she didn't care. Didn't care that she was half-naked in the window, being groped from behind by a fully clothed man like some debauched scene in a Renaissance painting.

She was here for a few blissful days with this man and no one knew or cared who she was. Or even where she was, for that matter. Apart from her security detail, of course.

'Still time to switch the window,' he whispered, his breath hot in her ear as the car drew closer, her nipples now clamped between dual pincer grips, one meaty quad pressing between her legs, parting her thighs.

'No,' she repeated as she ground back into his thigh.

Reaching behind, Xiomara pulled her dress out from where his knee was pinning it to her body, gathering it up to give him access to the back. He muttered something low and dirty as the skirt cleared her ass to reveal the lacy T of her thong and two bare cheeks. He unhanded her temporarily to squeeze those cheeks, her breasts falling softly, the air abrading her excruciatingly sensitive nipples causing her to whimper.

'You have the most perfect ass,' he muttered, palming the flesh as he used his foot to widen her stance, nudging her legs apart, hitching her higher against the thick thrust of his leg. His hands grabbed her hips and pulled them back a little, hinging her slightly forward, driving the rim of his kneecap into the heat between her legs.

Xiomara gasped at the exquisite torment, her arms slipping from his neck to splay on the sill,

140 FORBIDDEN FLING WITH THE PRINCESS

her hair tumbling forward, her breasts swinging with the movement as the car passed by.

Did they see her, exposed and aroused, her red mouth gaping open?

She didn't know. She didn't care. All she could feel was him surrounding her, touching her, her pulse a drum in her chest and a hammer through her ears.

'Edmund,' she gasped as she flexed her hips, riding the thick nudge of his leg, her eyes shutting at the delicious sensations swamping her body, the free swing of her breasts an erotic kind of torment. 'Please.'

His knee jammed high and hard against her, pinning her to the sill as his hands left her hips. Xiomara moaned in protest but just as quickly they were back in place, his fingers branding the soft, round flesh as his wallet landed on the sill beside her hand.

'Condom.'

It wasn't a request—it was an imperative. A sexy, gravelly one that had Xiomara moving automatically to comply, her lungs heavy as wet sand, her hands shaking. Somehow, she found the dexterity to both open his wallet and locate a foil packet although she didn't know how as his knee kept up a maddeningly relentless grind as she tore the packet open with her teeth and shoved it behind her in his general direction.

He took it, easing his leg from between hers,

AMY ANDREWS 141

her heart slamming in her chest, her desire building with every rapid-fire rat-a-tat of her pulse as she waited.

And waited.

Didn't he *burn* like she was? Didn't he know she needed him inside her *now*?

Finally, she heard the metallic give of his zip and it was too much, she needed to touch him. Reaching behind, she knocked his hand away, seeking him out, her eager fingers breaching his underwear and hitting pay dirt, a triumphant sound tumbling from her parted mouth as she grasped his erection and brought it out to play.

'*Xio.*' His forehead thunked against the back of her head as she stroked up and down the satiny length of him, revelling in the thick, steely core. 'I can't think when you do that.'

Xiomara moaned at both the feel of him and the thick note of arousal she heard in his voice. She hoped he didn't think *she* was capable of coherent thought because she wasn't. She was just following the backbeat of lust thrumming through her system.

'Edmund.' She rolled back into him, rubbing herself along his shaft, her desire for him evident in her slickness. 'I need you now.'

Another unintelligible mumble fell from his throat as he knocked her hand aside, his knuckles grazing her ass. Xiomara moaned, splaying her hands on the sill again as her knees threatened

142 FORBIDDEN FLING WITH THE PRINCESS

to give out. But then he was done, lining himself up behind her as he yanked aside the lacy strip of nothing masquerading as underwear with one hand and jerked her hips back with the other, lifting her high on her toes.

He thrust then, in one quick move, entering her with a decisive stroke that tore the breath from her lungs and rocked her forward, her breasts swinging, her elbow giving out. Reaching for the windowpane for purchase, she flattened her palm against it, crying out at the pure unadulterated ecstasy of his complete possession.

No other man had ever *owned* her the way he did.

Before she could catch her breath, his hand slid onto her jaw, turning her head to his mouth, kissing her, hot and hard and wet, his tongue licking the seam of her lips, seeking entry as he withdrew from her body, being granted it as he plunged back inside, swallowing her gasp as his hand moved to the back of her thigh, urging it *up, up, up* until her knee rested on the windowsill, opening her completely to him as he slid in and out for a third time, her new position allowing him *deeper.*

Tearing her mouth from his, Xiomara gasped at the depth, at the way his girth stretched her and his length tested her uppermost limits. 'Edmund…' she moaned, barely able to drag her eyelids open from the pulse of pleasure kicking off deep and low. 'I…you… I…'

He chuckled at her incoherent mumbling, his breath hot on her neck. 'You want some more, Xio?' He didn't withdraw, he just *flexed* his hips in a grinding motion as his spare hand slid over the top of the palm she had flattened against the windowpane, his fingers interlinking with hers. 'Can you take me deeper?'

Xiomara moaned at the intimate pressure, her eyelids shuttering, lights popping behind. She was pretty sure Edmund had gone as far as he could, but if she had any more it was his. 'Deeper,' she muttered, her voice not much more than a ragged pant. 'More.'

The hand that held her thigh moved then, pressing between her shoulder blades, urging her down until her torso hovered off the sill, her stiff nipples lightly grazing the not-quite-smooth plasterwork, her hips angled even further until she was practically en pointe.

He withdrew then and thrust again, filling her once more, her body jerking with the action, her curls spiralling in disarray. Xiomara cried out at the erotic rub of her nipples against the sill. '*Yes*,' she said on a moan. 'Yes. Like that.'

And he gave it to her *like that*. There in the window of the cottage on the hill, looking over the clifftops and the sea and the town—not that she was conscious of any of it—thrusting and rocking and pounding, stoking and stoking until one tiny pinpoint of pleasure suddenly erupted into a

144 FORBIDDEN FLING WITH THE PRINCESS

wide crevasse of liquid bliss and she was pulled into it, clenching tight around him, dragging him into the fissure and drowning with him together.

At some point the pleasure receded and Edmund collapsed against her, the thump of his heart perfectly aligned with the thump of hers, his uneven breath hot in her hair as they lay there against the windowsill, joined in the most intimate way possible, exhausted but sated.

Xiomara stirred first as Edmund's body grew heavier and heavier in the drowsy post-coital haze, levering herself up onto her forearms.

'Sorry,' he murmured, his gravelly voice making her smile because *she'd* been the one to make him sound so thoroughly sated. 'I'm squashing you.' He kissed her bare shoulder blade as he also levered himself up, not separating from her but rising onto his palms, taking his own weight.

It made it easier to breathe but, perversely, she missed the intimacy of his dead weight.

Xiomara shut her eyes as his lips nuzzled her hair then drifted down her nape. 'I didn't know you were an exhibitionist,' he murmured, his warm breath ruffling the fine hairs there.

She laughed. 'I'm not.' Only with him, apparently.

'Did you want to go into St Ives?'

Xiomara did not. As soon as her legs returned to some semblance of normal control, she wanted to go to bed, directly to bed, and spend the rest of the day doing exactly *this* with this guy she couldn't seem to get enough of.

'Maybe tomorrow?'

She could feel his mouth curving against her skin as he dropped a kiss near her ear and murmured, 'Good answer.'

CHAPTER EIGHT

AFTER A LONG night twisting up the sheets, Xiomara woke late to the aroma of coffee as a steaming mug was placed on her bedside table.

'Morning, sleepyhead.' Edmund's low voice rumbled near her ear as he dropped a kiss on her bare shoulder. 'Sit up, I prepared some breakfast.'

Xiomara smiled to herself as she did his bidding, internal muscles protesting a little at the movement, causing her smile to widen. She caught a glimpse of his naked back and legs and taut buttocks clad only in boxer briefs as he disappeared from view and sighed happily.

This mini-break had been a *very* good idea.

He was back seconds later, tray in hands, affording her a front view, which was just as magnificent. 'Eggs, toast and fruit,' he exclaimed, striding towards her looking deliciously rumpled.

'Good in bed and the kitchen,' she teased.

Laughing, he deposited the tray on her lap. 'I'm a man of many talents.'

Yes, he was. Surgeon extraordinaire. Accomplished lover. Chef. And—she glanced at what appeared to be a crystal shot glass on the tray that had been transformed into a vase boasting four yellow and white wildflowers—florist.

Oh. Her heart gave a funny little twist in her chest. 'You picked me flowers,' she murmured, stroking the petals as she glanced up at him.

Xiomara had been the recipient of many flowers over the years. They had been delivered to her from all kinds of people for all kinds of reasons—usually flattery or favour—not to mention the fact she was surrounded by them in the palace every day. Vases of them everywhere sourced from the renowned royal gardens.

But these four simple wildflowers touched her deeper than any arty floral display.

He shrugged. 'They reminded me of you at the window yesterday. Beautiful. And free.'

Xiomara's breath hitched at the statement as simple as the flowers and yet somehow managing to wrap around her like a warm hug.

'Thank you,' she whispered.

Smiling, he touched her cheek gently for a brief moment before his hand fell away. 'Eat up, the sun is shining and the day is ours.'

The hug intensified. Xiomara liked the sound of that very much.

It was a fifteen-minute stroll into St Ives, where they delighted in playing tourist.

Xiomara wore a white cotton kaftan-style dress that flowed loosely around her body with cute,

148 FORBIDDEN FLING WITH THE PRINCESS

boho, crotchet trim around the flutter sleeves and the deep V of the neckline. With it she'd teemed a pair of tortoiseshell Cartier sunglasses and a colourful red scarf to secure her hair back in a ponytail at her nape. Edmund wore a white shirt and the floral print board shorts from the Seychelles.

Xiomara couldn't help but feel they looked like a couple who'd been together for ever instead of having only known each other for just over a week, which was fanciful, she knew, but made her feel all warm and glowy inside, anyway.

They walked to the end of Smeaton's Pier, dodging people, cars and stacks of lobster pots to take a selfie in front of the white-washed lighthouse on the end. They ducked in and out of the artisan shops along Wharf Road and Fore Street, selling everything from clothes to handicrafts to candy.

Xiomara bought a silver necklace sporting a large piece of amber sea glass. It reminded her of Edmund's eyes and the woman who sold it to her had not only crafted it herself but had also picked up the piece of glass on nearby Porthmeor Beach. Edmund helped her put it on, the glass pendant sitting snug just above her cleavage, and Xiomara knew she would treasure it always.

She might have access to the Castilonian crown jewels and always took care to wear jewellery by local Castilonian artisans when on official duties, but this piece would forever remind her of St Ives and the guy who'd somehow managed to steal a little piece of her heart in such a short amount of time.

Once they'd explored all the galleries and shops and with the tide on its way out, they strolled hand in hand along the harbour beach, the calm water occasionally lapping at their feet. They licked ice cream cones as they dodged the throngs of holidaymakers, mostly young families enjoying the sunny weather that was, according to Edmund, ridiculously unusual. Apparently, summer weather in the UK wasn't as predictable as it was in the Mediterranean.

'This has been a great day,' she said as she popped the tip of the cone in her mouth and crunched.

'It has, hasn't it?' Edmund agreed, sliding his arm around her shoulder, kissing her upturned nose without breaking stride.

Xiomara's heart filled so big in her chest she was afraid it might bust right out. Her life had been packed full of amazing life experiences—people, places, things—and she was grateful for the privilege, but they had only enhanced her appreciation for the simple joys.

She knew they were often the sweetest and this day was no exception.

A toddler ambled drunkenly into their path. She was wearing a pink and purple swim shirt that covered all the way to her wrists, swim pants with three rows of ruffles on the butt and a white bucket

150   FORBIDDEN FLING WITH THE PRINCESS

hat perched at a precarious angle on her head as if she'd attempted to take it off then abandoned the action in favour of a stroll. Or rather, a totter.

Xiomara smiled as she and Edmund, their hands still clasped, separated to avoid a collision, allowing the little girl to pass between them, but somehow, she managed to stumble and overbalance anyway, plopping to the sand on her frilled bottom.

'Upsy-daisy,' Xiomara said as she dropped Edmund's hand to crouch down to check the little girl was okay. The hem of her kaftan was getting wet and sandy but she didn't care.

The cherub-cheeked little one stared at her with great affront, her bottom lip quivering as if her ignominious fall had been a huge insult to her ego.

'Oh, hey there, little one,' Xiomara crooned. 'No need to cry. The sun is shining and you are ah-dorable.' She smiled as she gently straightened the skew-whiff hat on the toddler's head. 'Here—' she held out her hand '—I'll help you up if you like.'

The wobbly bottom lip stopped as the toddler looked at Xiomara's hand curiously then at Xiomara for long solemn moments before breaking into a gappy grin and putting her arms out in the universal sign for *pick me up*.

Xiomara laughed. How could she resist that?

Pushing to her feet, Xiomara took both the toddler's hands and gently pulled her off the sand and back onto her wobbly legs. 'Where's your mama and papa?' she asked, looking around at the crowds of people, trying to see if anyone was looking for a runaway toddler.

'I think that's them,' Edmund said, pointing to two frantic people pushing through the clumps of beachgoers, rushing towards them.

The woman was upon them in seconds, scooping the toddler up and hugging the child to her fiercely, pressing kisses to her temple muttering, 'Thank God, thank God, thank God...'

The little girl, clearly unconcerned by the frantic reunion, squirmed in her hold.

'Hey,' said the guy who pulled up seconds later, looking just as harried as the woman. He put his hand out to Edmund and they shook. 'Sorry...we just turned our back and my wife thought I was looking out for her and I thought she was looking out for her and she...was just gone.'

The little girl held out her arms to the man and said, 'Dada.'

He smiled at his daughter and took her, slipping an arm around his wife's shoulder and planting a kiss on the top of her head as they huddled together for a moment.

'Thank you so much,' the woman said after a moment, her voice tremulous. 'Don't ever have kids, you two, they'll give you grey hairs.'

Xiomara glanced awkwardly at Edmund, cringing internally at the woman's assumption, about to rush in and explain that they weren't together like that in case Edmund felt put on the spot or

152   FORBIDDEN FLING WITH THE PRINCESS

embarrassed, but he just laughed and said, 'We'll take that on board.'

Which caused a funny little hitch in Xiomara's pulse.

The couple moved off, the toddler waving a pudgy little hand at them, and she and Edmund laughed as they resumed their stroll, his hand sliding into hers once again. 'You were good with her,' he said.

Xiomara glanced at him, surprised. She'd expected the conversation might be a little stilted after the mother's incorrect conclusion as to their relationship status. Or that he'd avoid any mention of the incident.

'I think it's the accent,' she said dismissively.

'You want to have children?'

Okay…he *was* going to go there.

'Yes,' she said simply. She wanted children. With the right man. There'd been too many *suitable* men pushed in her direction to not want *the one* for her baby daddy.

'And…you?' she asked tentatively.

She thought he might demur. He did not.

'It's complicated for me,' he admitted as he popped the last of his cone in his mouth, crunching and swallowing before he continued. 'I grew up in areas where poverty was everywhere. Babies, little children, their mothers, trying to eke out an existence in famines and wars.' He shrugged. 'That tends to skew a person's view. I think the world population is hugely problematic for sustaining the planet and it's an issue that's only going to get worse, and that worries me.'

Xiomara knew from her background research that Edmund had grown up in a world of famines and wars so it made sense that he would have a very different perspective. It sounded as if there was a *but* though. Otherwise, it wouldn't be complicated. It'd just be *no children* and he wouldn't have a problem with it because she'd learned that about him the past week.

He was decisive.

'But?'

'But… I see parents every day in what I do who are fighting tooth and nail for their baby. Or babies. I see new life come into the world all the time and it always hits me in the chest. The incredible wondrousness of it all. And I understand that as humans we have a basic drive to procreate.' He shrugged. 'I just…don't seem to feel that for myself. Or I haven't anyway. When I think about my life, I think about all the things I can do as a doctor, the people I can help. The technologies and possibilities of the future. It sounds conceited, I guess, but that's what excites me, drives me, and I worry that there isn't room for anything else.'

Xiomara heard the passion in his voice for his work and knew enough about his career to understand that the world needed people like Edmund Butler. But she still heard that note of uncertainty

154 FORBIDDEN FLING WITH THE PRINCESS

as if maybe he was trying to convince himself. Or wasn't as sure as he liked to be.

And that was possibly something new?

He gave a self-deprecating laugh as they avoided several seagulls fighting over a chip that had been tossed in their direction. 'I told you it was complicated.'

He wasn't on his lonesome there.

'It's complicated for me, too.'

She slowed and then stopped as he turned to face her, their fingers still intertwined, a question in his eyes. 'How so?'

Xiomara stared at the ocean over his shoulder for a moment before focusing on him, her heart giving a funny little flip at his earnest attention. She wasn't used to being heard. For so long she had felt voiceless. 'Children just aren't children for me. They are *literally* the lifeblood of monarchy and I have been raised to be a...royal breeder.'

'That sounds like a lot of pressure.'

'Indeed.' She smiled at his understatement. 'Having babies because you *want* them and believe that they are the ultimate expression of love between two people doesn't exactly fit with the royal succession plan.'

Being a hopeless romantic had been difficult when she'd been born into a system that privileged pedigree over personality, lineage over love.

'I imagine the twins have eased that burden a little.'

She nodded. *Enormously.* 'Especially given they're boys.'

'Castilona has a male succession line?'

'Yes.' She gave him a wry smile. 'We have not yet caught up with your British royals, who changed that rule.'

'Seems to me that kind of change might be something a new young monarch might be able to effect.'

'Indeed.' Xiomara smiled again.

It certainly would never have happened under her father's rule. Tavi had ascended the throne with many things to do to set the house of de la Rosa in order and had accomplished much in his short reign. Laws of succession had been way down on the list but it was something she planned to raise with him once he'd settled into his role.

After his sons were born.

Not because she ever wanted to be Queen herself but because, had there been a scenario where she was thrust into the position, she could have just as ably ruled as any man.

Xiomara started to walk again, their hands still clasped. 'Is that why you split with your fiancée?' she asked as the question came to mind. 'Did she want children?'

Given his eyebrow raise, it was perhaps a question she shouldn't have let out without proper examination. *Well done, Xiomara.* Still, she had been curious about the woman since she'd read the factoid in the report. For a moment she thought she might have erred but then he chuckled.

'I keep forgetting you have this secret dossier on me.'

She laughed. It was hardly secret. But the question was out there now and she was dying to know the answer.

'That was some of the reason, yes,' he admitted.

'And the rest?' It was none of her business, but Xiomara couldn't stop now.

'I was twenty-four. Kelly wanted a much smaller life. And I don't mean that in a condescending way. She's a good person who knew what she wanted. A house in the suburbs, two kids and a dog. But I was driven even then, eager to see where my career might take me and none of it involved her vision. Not at twenty-four, anyway. At that point I was still thinking maybe I'd follow in my parents' footsteps and she definitely wasn't keen on that.'

'So why get engaged?'

'It was a mistake. We'd been together for a few years and known each other for much longer and all our friends were getting engaged and her expectation was that we'd be next and it *did* seem like the next logical step so I took it. But then I worked a shift in the emergency department where a woman with a twin pregnancy presented at twenty-four weeks with TTTS and one of the babies had already died, which was—'

He shook his head, his features suddenly bleak

as if he was right back there again instead of on a Cornish beach on a sunny summer's day, and Xiomara's stomach dropped, thinking about Tavi and Phoebe's twins.

'Just so, *so* tragic,' he continued. 'And a couple of months later an opportunity came up for me to intensively study placental vasculature in the US for three months and I could feel in my bones that I was *meant* to do it, that I *had* to. Like a calling. Like my parents had felt called to humanitarian work. Kelly didn't want to leave and she didn't want me to go either and I suddenly felt...*caged*. So, I broke it off, which was about as awful as you can imagine and hurt her incredibly.'

A heavy layer of regret laced Edmund's voice and Xiomara could sense it had been a turbulent time for him. Clearly not something he'd done lightly and still felt remorse over. But the incident with the twin pregnancy had clearly affected him and knowing what she knew about him, witnessing how his skills and knowledge had saved her cousin's two unborn babies *because* of the path he'd chosen, she was grateful he'd felt compelled to follow his *calling*.

She squeezed his hand but didn't say anything and they walked in silence for a beat or two before he spoke again. 'What about you?' He glanced at her. 'Anyone serious in your past? I imagine it's not just any guy who can date a princess.'

158   FORBIDDEN FLING WITH THE PRINCESS

'Well, *theoretically*, anyone can. It's just… harder in practice.'

He laughed. 'I can only imagine.'

'And it…can be hard to know who's genuine, even amongst my peers. So… I'm usually fairly cautious with men.'

She hadn't been with him though. She'd thrown herself into this—fling? liaison? flirtation?—headlong. Maybe because she'd realised straight from the get-go that Edmund Butler wasn't like any other man she'd ever met. He was a *unicorn*. And a woman from her world could only ever have one chance with a guy like him.

'That sounds both wise and a little sad.'

'And my father, of course, had his own ideas about suitable matches for me.'

His brow crinkled. 'What do you mean, suitable?'

'A match that would advance Castilona's interests. Joining two royal houses together through marriage and then, of course, linking them permanently, through children.'

'Okay…' Edmund gave a half laugh that reeked of disbelief, as if he might just have stepped into an alternate reality.

Except it was *her* life.

'That sounds very *Game of Thrones*.'

Xiomara laughed at the analogy. 'Kind of, yes. Thankfully, my mother vetoed them all. Which is why—' she let go of his hand and spun around

AMY ANDREWS 159

slowly a couple of times as she walked, turning her face to the sun '—I get to be with you, here.'

She really didn't want to talk about the convoluted nature of her life any more. Not today. Not on this beach in this beautiful place. Not with him. Her father's constant interference was in the past and she didn't want to besmirch the memory of this place with thoughts of him.

Taking the hint, Edmund tucked her into his side. 'What say we head up there—' he tipped his chin to the area where several cafés and bars beckoned from beneath colourful awnings and tall glasses of orange drinks glowed in the sunshine '—get us one of those fancy drinks and watch the world go by?'

'I think that sounds perfect.'

Edmund was about as relaxed as he'd been that day in the Seychelles before Xiomara had swooped in and completely disrupted his peace—in more ways than one. Sure, this was a busy street café in a bustling Cornish seaside town in high summer, not a secluded Seychelles beach. But the knowledge he got to spend these next few days just enjoying this woman's company was surprisingly more restful than any seclusion.

She was fun and funny, engaging, articulate and bright. And so, so sexy. She was incredibly tactile and playful and eager, with a confidence in her body and the way she moved that was both sensual and bodacious. And refreshing. In his experience, too many women today were dissatisfied with their bodies to some degree or other and he'd have expected a woman who had grown up in front of the paparazzi to be even more so.

Especially one who was soft and curvy with hips and thighs and boobs in a world where *skinny* was fashionable and anyone with a keyboard could be a critic.

But Xiomara de la Rosa seemed inordinately comfortable in her skin.

Maybe that came from her innate privilege. Being able to afford anything you desired to look and feel good about yourself and the luxury of people kissing your ass all day. Whatever it was, Ed was here for it because just being around her was relaxing.

He didn't feel as if he was just marking time when he was in her company. The constant drive to push himself quietened in her presence. That might have terrified him a week ago, but today he revelled in it.

Revelled in this *thing* between them. That had been there since the Seychelles. That he didn't think he'd ever felt with another woman and made him exceptionally grateful her father had never succeeded in his attempts to marry her off.

A *suitable* guy?

Xiomara deserved someone of intellect and passion, not lineage and position.

He was almost at the bottom of his Aperol when Xiomara's phone rang and her eyes widened in alarm as she glanced at the screen, which yanked him out of his relaxation by the roots of his hair.

'It's Tavi.'

The apprehension in her voice was echoed in the sudden double beat of his heart. Octavio, wanting his cousin to completely get away from it all, had promised phone silence—so had her security—but they had insisted Xiomara have her mobile on at all times for tracking purposes, which she'd complied with more than happily.

So, something had to be wrong. Was it Phoebe? And, if so, why hadn't the King called Ed? He had insisted Octavio call him if there were any concerns regarding the Queen's health. Had he been trying to call and not been able to get through? Ed checked his phone as Xiomara answered hers.

'Tavi?' Xiomara's high voice betrayed her anxiety. 'What's wrong? Is it Phoebe?'

Ed was only privy to one side of the conversation but it was quickly evident, by the way Xiomara's shoulders dropped and the look of relief sweeping across her face, that Phoebe was fine.

'*No* way.' Xiomara glanced at him, irritation flashing in the flecks of her eyes.

'What's wrong?' he mouthed.

She shook her head at him as she said, 'But how?' And then she dropped her face into her hand and rubbed her forehead. 'Okay…yes…okay. Send

162 FORBIDDEN FLING WITH THE PRINCESS

them through. Okay… Ask Xavier to give me half an hour before he calls?' She nodded a couple of times. 'Uh-huh… Yes, thanks. Talk soon.'

A harsh exhaled breath ruffled a couple of curls that had escaped the red scarf tied at her nape to bounce around her forehead. She shot him an apologetic look. 'I'm so sorry, Edmund,' she murmured. 'The game is up.'

Ed frowned. 'What does that mean? What's he sending through?'

Her phone chimed then and she held up a finger as she scrolled on her screen. Despite her annoyance and irritation, Ed couldn't help but smile. She was used to having that finger obeyed and the temptation to lean in and suck it into his mouth was a living breathing beast inside him, but her softly muttered, 'Oh, no…' cut it off at the knees.

Sliding his hand across the table to cover hers, he said, 'What? Now you're worrying me.'

Reluctantly, she passed the phone across the table and Ed picked it up with his spare hand. There on the screen was the front page of a well-known tabloid. And he was on it.

What the hell?

It was a little grainy, clearly taken with a telephoto lens, but definitely him. It wasn't the first time Ed had ever been in a newspaper—not by a long shot. Over the course of his career there had been many articles written about him. So much so the Institute had a press kit on their website for media to easily access carefully curated images of himself both formally and in a work setting.

This was not that. This was the first time he'd been in a newspaper kissing a woman. Under a headline that screamed: *The Princess and the Posh Doc!*

'What the hell?' he said, aloud this time, as he looked up from the phone.

'Yep.'

'Is that the—' Ed scrutinized the picture a little closer. 'That's the hospital car park, the morning after we...' It was hard to believe it was only three days ago.

'Yep.'

'But there were no paparazzi around when we arrived.'

'It seemed that way. But I should have known. There's always one. I'm sorry I was a little too...'

Ed glanced up as her voice trailed off. Her cheeks were glowing and she was biting her bottom lip. He quirked an eyebrow as he interlinked his fingers with hers. 'A little too...?'

He knew exactly what *a little too* she was. A little too *sexed up.* Just as he had been. A little too full of all the intimate new things they'd discovered about each other swirling between them on residual heat and hormones.

'Distracted,' she said, with a twitch of her lips.

'Yeah.' Ed grinned. 'Me too.'

He supposed it was wrong to be grinning at each

164   FORBIDDEN FLING WITH THE PRINCESS

other in this situation, but he was right back at that kiss and he was pretty sure he'd have still kissed her in that moment whether he'd known they were being watched or not.

Staring at him for a beat or two longer, she murmured, 'There's more. Swipe left.'

Two more images confronted him on the next two screens. One was him leaving the hospital the day he'd done the laser surgery on the twins. The other was of Xiomara on the same day, being sneaked out of the back entrance by her security. The photographers had managed to get a decent shot of her—decent enough to support the gist of the article.

Ed scanned the article. It had apparently not gone unnoticed that the *royal clothes horse of Castilona* was in the same outfit both days. From that and the car park kiss the next morning, they had come to the very accurate conclusion that Xiomara must have stayed the night with the doctor that had performed *heroic lifesaving treatment on the royal heirs.*

The statement that had been released yesterday from the King and Queen hadn't named Ed as the doctor or even the TTTS specifics but, given the picture of him and Xiomara kissing in the car park the morning after, they had definitely joined all the dots.

One part of Ed admired the way they'd put the *story* together. They'd obviously had to do some

AMY ANDREWS 165

digging to identify him then piece together the car park kiss, the hospital and the royal statement to figure out the full picture. The tone was ridiculously sensationalist and exceptionally unkind—*royal clothes horse* indeed—but they had essentially got it right.

'Okay.' He handed the phone back. 'So, what do we do?'

She blinked. 'You're not freaked out?'

'That I'm on the front page of a paper kissing a beautiful woman who knocked on my door the day before with ravage-ment on her mind?'

Her cheeks warmed some more as she fought the urge to smile, and hell if that didn't give his heart a little kickstart. 'I'm being serious.'

'Sorry.' He smiled at her, not remotely sorry. Hell if he didn't want to kiss her right now. 'It is what it is, I guess. I'm more concerned about what it means for you.'

'Well…the hunt will be on now, that's for sure. Every pap in the country will be trying to figure out where we are. There'll be a bounty on our heads.'

'Okay, but…' He shrugged. 'None of them know we're here, right?'

'No. But Xavier will be calling soon and I'm pretty sure he'll try to talk me into coming back. Or him coming here anyway. He takes his job very seriously.'

'Of course he does. I'm *glad* he does. But I re-

166   FORBIDDEN FLING WITH THE PRINCESS

peat: none of them know we're here. And I doubt any of them are going to think "let's go to Cornwall just in case". We're probably safer way down here in the West Country than in London.'

'You'll be surprised how they can ferret things out, the tricks they use. And with the pictures in every gossip mag and news site, it won't just be the paps to worry about. The public might notice us now too.'

Ed looked around at the café, where not one single person was paying them any attention. The only thing they appeared fixated on was the food, the sunshine and that view.

'So…' He shrugged. If she thought he was going to let this spoil their time together, she was wrong. He'd already had one break cut short; he wasn't going to let it happen again. 'We'll be careful.'

'Edmund.' She sighed and it was one of deep forbearance. This was obviously not her first rodeo. 'You don't know these people.'

Maybe he didn't know them personally, but the British people knew intimately how persistent they could be and how their antics to get that one perfect picture could endanger people's lives. And this was the reality for Xiomara and it made him want to break things at the thought of how it *narrowed* her life.

Sure, on the outside she appeared to have enormous privilege and freedom, but in reality, she was attached to a gilded retractable leash that was only so long before it yanked her back.

'Do you feel unsafe here with me?' This seemed to be a paparazzi issue only, not some legitimate threat to her life from someone who would do her harm. That was an entirely different matter and Ed would happily go back or move Xavier onto the couch at the cottage.

Whatever she wanted.

'No.' Her fingers tightened around his. 'Absolutely not.'

'Do you *want* to go back?' If she wanted that, then of course they'd leave immediately.

Slowly, she shook her head. 'No.'

Ed smiled. 'Why don't I duck back to that shop from earlier and buy you that enormous floppy hat you tried on?'

She regarded him for a few moments as if she was seriously considering his proposal, a smile slowly curving the plush red outline of her mouth. 'We should probably lie low for a day or so.'

'Oh, no.' Ed clutched his heart as he feigned disappointment. 'Whatever will we do?'

CHAPTER NINE

ED WAS AWARE that Xavier wasn't very happy with their plan to lie low and stick it out in Cornwall, although he had conceded it was probably less visible than being in the capital. Surprisingly, Ed wasn't as irritated by Xiomara's pedantic security guy as he would have thought. He was comforted knowing that long after their time together was a faint memory, Xiomara would be safe, that someone had her back.

And in the meantime, he had Xiomara all to himself.

*Un*surprisingly, they had no problem filling the next day inside the cottage. The weather had turned overnight, becoming cool and blustery— so much for summer! But the change made it conducive to staying in bed and they burned up the sheets as the wind howled around the cottage and the rain lashed the windowpanes.

Although the sheets weren't the only things being burned…

He and Xiomara took advantage of the couch *and the* rug perfectly positioned in front of the roaring fire in the inglenook. The shower got a workout too, as did the bath, the floor a puddle of water by the time they were spent.

Finally, at almost ten p.m., they emerged for a proper meal, suddenly ravenous from a day of… not a lot of eating. With a supply of gourmet food that would probably outlast a small apocalypse there was plenty of choice, but they decided to keep it simple as they worked side by side preparing the meal.

'I'm impressed you know how to cook,' Ed murmured as he sliced an onion in nothing but his underwear. The cottage was cosy so there was no need to rug up.

She laughed as she cut fat slices of bread. 'I wouldn't get too excited. It's just a toasted cheese sandwich.'

'*Gourmet* cheese, artisan *sourdough* bread *and* onion,' he corrected. 'And anyway, I love a cheese toastie.'

'Me too.'

Hallelujah to that. The last woman he'd dated had avoided meat, dairy, gluten, sugar and carbs. Not because she was allergic but because she thought it was *healthy*. As a doctor, Ed knew that wasn't true and it made eating out a nightmare but she'd been cool and interesting and arty and not looking for anything long-term and he'd enjoyed her company otherwise.

Then she'd started commenting on his food choices when they dined out, which generally

170   FORBIDDEN FLING WITH THE PRINCESS

goaded him into choosing the most unhealthy things he could find and he realised life was too short for such passive-aggressive crap and that no amount of cool, interesting, arty and commitment-phobia could compensate for silent judgement over his medium rare steak.

Picking up her glass of wine, Xiomara took a sip, the orange flame of the fire in the background causing it to glow a deep ruby red. 'I used to love visiting the palace kitchens as a kid,' she said. 'The head cook—Carlota—she's Xavier's mother, she was an absolute wizard.'

Ed raised an eyebrow. 'You knew Xavier before he was on your detail?'

'Not really, no. I caught sight of him a few times as a kid but he's older than me so we never really met properly. Although Carlota used to talk about him all the time. Anyway…' Xiomara continued '…*she* could make the most amazing delicacies and put on a meal at short notice for impromptu guests without breaking a sweat. But she always said mastering the art of a *toastie*—' he smiled at how her accent imbued the humble dish with a Mediterranean *je ne sais quoi* '—was a skill all people should have up their sleeves. And she taught me her secret.'

'Oh, yeah?' Ed put down the knife as he slid in behind her, placing his hands either side of the bench, caging her between the hardness of the stone top and the hardness of his erection. She hummed appreciatively as her hair tickled his face. 'What's that?'

'Thick bread. Fresh herbs. Don't skimp on the butter.'

'Or the cheese, by the looks of it,' he murmured as he took in the thick, fragrant slabs of the Keltic Gold sitting next to the fresh thyme on the cutting board.

'Well, if you're going to have a cheese toastie, there's no point skimping on the cheese.'

Ed couldn't agree more. 'Hear, hear,' he muttered as he nuzzled the side of her neck, rubbing against her, the shiver that raised goosebumps down her neck passing straight through him as well.

He was all for no skimping when it came to food. Or other pleasures of the flesh.

From his vantage point he could see straight down her shirt. Or *his* shirt as the case might be. It was from his old alma mater and had been with him since his first year at Cambridge. It covered enough of her to be considered decent—sitting just under the curve of her ass cheeks—but there was nothing decent about Xiomara in his shirt, the sea glass pendant sitting temptingly at the V of her cleavage. And he knew for a fact she was wearing no panties.

She looked sinfully, decadently indecent.

'That T-shirt looks far better on you than it does on me,' he mused, noting the way her hardening

172 FORBIDDEN FLING WITH THE PRINCESS

nipples beaded against the fabric as she layered up the sourdough.

'In that case, you won't mind if I keep it?'

Ordinarily, Ed *would* mind very much. The shirt was a favourite, worn soft and thin over the years. But the thought that Xiomara would be somewhere in the world, wearing his T-shirt? Yeah, that was worth the sacrifice.

'It's all yours.'

Right now, though, as the insatiable need to touch her rode him again, his only interest in his shirt was getting her out of it as quickly as possible. Removing one hand from the bench, he slid it down between her thighs, where he found her bare and wet and ready.

'Edmund…' she gasped, gripping the bench '…the toasties.'

'What about them?' He stroked her as he bit gently into the slope where her neck met her shoulder.

She moaned as his other hand slid under her shirt and moved north, cupping a breast, teasing the nipple. 'I thought you were hungry?'

'I am.' Unhanding her long enough to spin her around, he ravaged her mouth as he pushed the cutting board aside and urged her up onto the kitchen bench. 'Very hungry,' he muttered as he broke the kiss, sliding the shirt up her thighs, exposing her to his view as he dropped into a crouch and feasted until she was drumming her heels on his back and crying out his name.

***

They stayed inside another day, the inclement weather conducive to the decision, but when the sun was shining the next morning they decided to venture out for a drive. Ed had been more than fine to stay inside again but Xiomara had taken one look at the blue sky and declared they *had* to get out for some fresh air. And Ed was happy they had as they left the seaside behind, driving at a leisurely pace from St Ives to the Lizard peninsula, stopping to stroll through quaint, less busy villages on the way.

They stopped at a thatched roof pub for lunch, where there were only a handful of people dining in the sunny beer garden, paying zero attention to the woman in the floppy white hat. Ed, on the other hand, couldn't take his eyes off her. There was something about Xiomara incognito and the way that she kept peeping at him from under the brim that was super sexy but also just…made his lungs feel too big for his chest.

It made him feel like he was the luckiest man in the world.

By mid-afternoon they were back at the beach but one of the less popular ones, not far from St Ives. There were only about a quarter of the people compared to three days ago, and fewer family groups given the surf was still up from the recent squalls despite the sunnier weather.

And nobody recognized them, so they just lazed

174   FORBIDDEN FLING WITH THE PRINCESS

in the sun on the towels they'd thrown in the boot this morning. With Xiomara's head on his chest, her curls brushing his chin, Ed shut his eyes and drifted off to sleep. There hadn't been a whole lot of sleep going on at the cottage—actually, since he and Xiomara had been sharing a bed—and the sound of the surf and seagulls and the warmth of the sun lulled him into a doze.

He wasn't sure how long he'd been asleep when he first heard the commotion but people yelling soon yanked him out of his slumber. For a disorientating moment, he thought someone had recognized Xiomara and he gathered her protectively in his arms as she also stirred. But then he realised there were people running towards the water. Towards a man who was running out of the ocean, calling for help as he carried a very floppy-looking child out of the waves.

It took no time at all for Ed's medical instincts to kick in and he shot to his feet, quickly covering the distance to where the rescuer had placed the child on the sand.

'Stand aside,' he ordered as he pushed through the small knot of people that had gathered around the child, the control he always felt in these situations taking hold. Adrenaline buzzed through his system but Ed knew how to hone it and use it to his advantage. 'I'm a doctor, stand aside.'

He was vaguely aware that Xiomara had followed him as the crowd parted and he knelt in the sand quickly, casting his eye over the child, who lay wet and shivering on the sand. He looked to be about eight or nine and had been placed on his side although not in any kind of useful way. He was breathing, but only just, his skinny shoulders shrugging as he coughed ineffectually and gasped like a fish, his lips dusky, his eyes wide with fright.

Ed felt for the carotid pulse, which was slow but present. 'Somebody call an ambulance,' he demanded.

'I will,' someone from the crowd said as the guy who had pulled the child from the surf grasped Ed's arm.

'Help him,' he begged. 'Please help him.'

'What happened?' Ed asked as he positioned the child correctly, lifting his chin for proper jaw support, which brought the airway into anatomical alignment and almost instantly improved the boy's breathing and the colour of his lips.

'He was there beside me one minute, we were only shallow, just jumping the waves. We were having fun. We do it all the time. He loves it. Then a big one hit and his hand was ripped from mine and I couldn't find him. Oh, God—' His voice cracked. 'Is he…did he drown?'

'No.' But he nearly had. And would have, had he not been found in time. The undertow could be deceptively strong after storms. 'I'd say he probably hit his head as the wave churned him around and knocked him out briefly. He probably inhaled some water. Are you his father?'

'Yes.'

'What's his name?'

'Alfie.'

'Okay, Alfie.' Ed lowered his head to murmur in the boy's ear as he gently stroked his wet hair with his spare hand. 'You've taken some water on board and you're a bit dazed but you're going to be okay now.'

'Ambulance is ten minutes away,' said a voice from behind somewhere.

Ed nodded. Barring unforeseen circumstances, Alfie would be okay, but he'd give anything for some oxygen and his stethoscope right now.

The child gave a weak cough, his shoulders shrugging with the effort as his father knelt over him. 'Hear that, Alfie? You're going to be fine. The ambulance is almost here.'

Ed felt for Alfie's pulse again, which was less bradycardic now. His skin was cold to touch however and goosebumps stippled the boy's flesh. He raised his head to ask for something to keep Alfie warm but it was already there.

'Here.'

He looked up to find Xiomara passing him her sun-warmed towel. 'Thank you,' he said, smiling at her as he handed it to Alfie's father to do the honours.

Ed noticed a few phones out taking snaps and

AMY ANDREWS

for a moment he thought it was to do with Xiomara, before he realised they were taking pictures of a prostrate Alfie. He frowned as he angled his body to block their shots. What on earth were they going to do with pictures like that? Put them on their social media?

'Okay, folks.' He looked around the concerned faces. 'Everything is under control now. Let's give the lad some privacy.'

The innate authority in his voice dispersed the crowd to a point. Most still watched the spectacle from close by, standing in small groups, clearly discussing what they'd just witnessed. Xiomara knelt beside him then as Alfie's father reached across and clasped Ed's shoulder. 'Thank you, thank you,' he said. 'I'm Raymond.'

'Ed. And this is Xiom… Xio.'

Not that Raymond noticed the stumble over her name as he stroked his son's head but Ed silently berated himself. Xiomara wasn't exactly a common name in the UK.

As if she knew he was beating himself up, she gave his arm a squeeze and smiled at him, mouthing, 'It's okay.'

'I'm so sorry to interrupt your day like this,' Raymond apologised to Xiomara as he glanced up from his boy. 'But I don't know what I would have done—' his voice cracked '—without your man, here.'

Your man. It had been less than two weeks and

178 FORBIDDEN FLING WITH THE PRINCESS

not exactly what was happening, but hell if Ed didn't like the sound of that.

'Please don't concern yourself about that,' Xiomara said in what Ed was coming to think of as her *princess* voice. Soothing, gracious, diplomatic. 'We're just grateful to have been in the right place at the right time.'

'Yes,' Ed agreed.

'Will he need to stay in hospital?' Raymond asked.

'I imagine they'll want to monitor him overnight,' Ed confirmed as a siren wailed in the distance.

Within five minutes, Ed was handing over to two paramedics as he assisted them with Alfie. They had an oxygen mask in place and Alfie on a monitor pronto. His heart rate was now within normal limits but his saturations had been in the low nineties prior to commencing the oxygen therapy. One of the paramedics loaned Ed a stethoscope and he listened to the boy's chest which was, as he suspected, full of crackles.

They'd definitely want to monitor him overnight with his lungs being so irritated from the seawater and the possibility of pulmonary oedema.

A few minutes later Ed and Xiomara, along with everyone else—and their phones—on the beach, watched as the paramedics stretchered Alfie, swaddled in a space blanket that reminded him of the dress Xiomara had been wearing during their first meeting, to the waiting ambulance. Raymond followed, holding his son's hand.

'My hero,' Xiomara murmured in his ear. 'You're kinda hot when you go all doctor.'

Ed grinned as he turned to look at her, dragging her close, his hands moving to her ass. 'You ought to talk, coming in there with the towel before I even asked for it, like a scrub nurse who knows exactly the right instrument to pass up at exactly the right time. That was very hot.'

He swooped in and kissed her, high on a combination of residual adrenaline, a good outcome and the scent and the taste of this woman who already seemed to be able to read his mind. Heat sparked between them that was really more appropriate for behind closed doors.

'Excuse me, mister?'

Reluctantly, Ed dragged his mouth off hers, although he didn't let go of Xiomara, his body still buzzing from their insane chemistry. Three teenage girls were looking at him curiously and had he had his wits about him, he might have been more wary than irritated. 'Yes?'

Clearly the leader of the trio, the teenager who'd addressed him stepped forward. 'Aren't you that couple that's been all over the news?'

Ed's heart skipped a beat as his awareness broadened out to the wider beach area, noticing people pointing and murmuring, their phones no

180 FORBIDDEN FLING WITH THE PRINCESS

longer trained on the ambulance in the parking area but on them.

'You're that Castilonian princess,' she continued, looking at Xiomara. 'And you're the doctor that saved the royal babies' lives?'

'No, no,' Xiomara denied in her unruffled princess voice even as she tensed in his arms.

Ignoring their denials, one of the other girls stepped forward. 'Could we get a picture?'

'Time to leave,' Xiomara murmured.

'Uh-huh,' Ed agreed as more phones came out.

'Sorry,' Xiomara said, easing out of his arms. 'We're on holiday. I'm sure you understand.'

She tugged on his hand then and Ed followed as they trudged to where they'd left their things, pausing only for him to quickly scoop them up and for Xiomara to cram the floppy hat on her head before they hurried off the beach.

Something disturbed Xiomara early the next morning as the first light of dawn broke through the window, although she wasn't sure what. Her body was loose and supple from another late night of naked times, the sheets twisted around her body. Edmund, lying on his belly and barely covered at all, had one arm flung across her stomach. It was heavy in his slumber but she smiled to herself, loving how good it felt, how possessive it felt pinning her to the mattress.

She stretched languorously, her muscles liquid, her body feeling as if she'd been marinated in heated honey, a warm glow in her chest.

The noise came again and she frowned, a sudden itch up her spine. It sounded distant. Maybe the patter of rain against the triple-glazed windowpane? The meteorological app had predicted more sunshine and, after their day had been cut short yesterday, she'd been hoping for continued fine weather for their trip to Bodmin, which they'd discussed last night.

After she had reported yesterday's incident to Xavier, he had suggested they lie low again in case the pictures taken on the beach managed to alert the paparazzi to their location. *And they would.* It was hardly going to be busy where they were going and they'd planned on taking a picnic lunch.

With them having to head back to London tomorrow for Phoebe's ultrasound, they only had one more full day together and she wanted to make the most of it.

They hadn't talked about what came next. They hadn't needed to. Because she'd go back to Castilona, where the planning for the Fiesta del Vino de Verano would be in full swing—as patron, Xiomara was heavily involved in its organisation. And Edmund would go to Africa and then back to his normal life doing important work. *Very* important work.

She was his holiday fling and everybody knew they didn't survive past the plane trip home.

182   FORBIDDEN FLING WITH THE PRINCESS

More pattering noises had Xiomara lifting her head off the bed. Unfortunately, what she found was *not* the wet splat of rain running down the glass but about a dozen photographers standing on the other side of the stone wall, merrily snapping pictures through their zoom lenses of her and Edmund through the window.

What. The. Hell.

'*Mierda*,' she cursed under her breath as a heavy knot of dread pulled taut in her stomach. '*Edmund*,' she whispered, although why she didn't know—it wasn't as if they could hear her outside. But she didn't want him to make any sudden movements and possibly give the paparazzi a full-frontal view of his naked form. For sure it was impressive but she was certain he didn't want the world to know what the renowned foetal surgeon was packing. She just needed him to reach out, grab the window remote that was on his bedside table and block those bloodsuckers out.

He stirred a little, his hand shifting from her stomach, moving south as he nuzzled her neck. The fine nerve-endings beneath her skin twitched as a familiar heat flared between her legs and she shut her eyes tight, fighting the urge to undulate into the treacherous slide of his hand.

Instead, she clamped down hard on it and, keeping her voice low, said, 'Edmund, I don't know how, but there's a bunch of guys out there with cameras taking pictures of us. Can you reach the window remote?'

Edmund's hand froze. She hadn't heard him say the four-letter word he muttered against her neck before but she couldn't agree more. The mattress shifted a little as he reached across the bed, groping for the remote. Xiomara could tell when it was done by the sounds of protest audible, if a little distant, through the triple glazing.

She blew out a breath. There went all their lovely peace and quiet.

Edmund levered himself up onto his elbows as he looked into her face, his eyes roving over her hair and her mouth before coming to lock with hers. 'I guess they found us, huh?'

'Yeah.' Xiomara grimaced. 'Sorry.'

His brow crinkled. 'How on earth did they find us at the cottage?'

Xiomara shook her head. 'I've given up working out how.' Being filmed and photographed at the beach was one thing, tracking them down here was entirely another. 'They've probably asked about us in town. Flashed our pictures around. Maybe someone from the other cottages along this lane recognized us?' They'd been out walking a couple of times and waved at people in passing cars who had waved at them.

Stroking his fingers down her neck, Edmund ran his thumb over the warm bulk of her sea glass pendant sitting pretty in the middle of her chest.

'Are they allowed to take pictures through the window like that?'

'Technically, no. But they're on the other side of the wall so they're not trespassing and we left the window uncovered so...'

'Yeah.'

He seemed as resigned as she was and Xiomara wanted to open the door and pelt eggs at the gutter press. *Damn it.* These past few days had been so incredibly fantastic and she wasn't ready for them to end. But she knew it was over. There'd never be able to shake them now. And the thought of them cooped up inside here with a bunch of photographers camped outside, idly speculating about what they were doing *and* how many times, made her skin crawl.

It had been nice while it lasted but it was over now.

'What do you want to do? How do we handle this?'

Xiomara sighed. 'I'll call Xavier. They'll come get me.'

'I can drive you back.'

'No.' Xiomara shook her head. 'The paps will follow us and it takes a special skill set to drive safely for yourself and everyone else whilst they're driving recklessly around you trying to get a good shot.'

Edmund didn't argue. He just nodded then dropped

his forehead to her chest, his breath warm on her cleavage.

'You should be able to get away okay. A few of them may hang around for a while after I leave, but I doubt they'll stick around for long.'

'Yeah,' he said, his voice a warm burr against her skin. 'I'll wait till the coast is clear.'

'I'm sorry,' she said again as she combed her fingers through his hair, staring at the ceiling, a heavy kind of wretchedness descending.

'Me too,' he murmured. 'Me too.'

CHAPTER TEN

THE TEXT CAME through to Xiomara's phone at five that afternoon, during a discussion she was having with Tavi and Phoebe about baby names.

Hey Xio. Finally home.

Xio… She blinked hard as the message went blurry and she fought a thickening in her throat. She was going to miss hearing him say that.

Xiomara shot back a quick reply.

Was traffic bad?

She'd thought he'd have been back in London hours ago.

Three little dots danced on her screen as he replied, his message landing within fifteen seconds.

The paps didn't leave until almost two. Don't know how you put up with them. You want to come over to the apartment? I also make a mean cheese toastie.

Xiomara's stomach dipped. *Don't know how you put up with them.* And therein lay the rub. She

AMY ANDREWS 187

didn't have a choice. In her world it was the cost of being born into a particular type of privilege.

To be fair, the interest was never usually this intense. She was, after all, just minor European royalty. But it always intensified if it looked like romance was on the cards.

The mere hint of some action for the Princess or, God forbid, an actual *boyfriend,* the paparazzi went into overdrive. And the last thing she wanted was for Edmund to have to endure that. Unfortunately, there was only one way to stop it and that was stop feeding the beast.

She replied with a heavy heart.

Can't. We're hosting a dinner here tonight for some innovation entrepreneurs wanting to invest in Castilonian viniculture.

It was a lie but she couldn't bear the thought of dragging it out. Their goodbye in Cornwall had been awkward enough. With the paparazzi at the front wall and Xavier and Felipe out in the living room, it had been about as intimate as a student house party.

Their little Cornish bubble had been resoundingly burst and maybe that was for the best.

She added to her text.

I'll see you tomorrow morning. At the ultrasound?

188   FORBIDDEN FLING WITH THE PRINCESS

And hit send.

It took ten minutes before his reply finally landed. In the meantime, those three tantalising little dots undulated before her eyes and despite Xiomara lecturing herself about being sensible and smart about the reality of their relationship, her hopes were buoyed.

Was he scripting an impassioned plea to keep seeing her? Hatching a plan to make it work between the two of them? Because God knew, she'd like that very much.

She'd expected some kind of tome for the amount of time it had taken but... no. It turned out he was not.

See you then.

Xiomara stared at those three little words until her eyeballs stung from not blinking. It was perverse to be feeling so devastated—she'd known him less than two weeks—to wish that he'd at least tried to rebuff her decision. But she couldn't help the way she felt. Which was why she should never have let herself get involved with someone *normal*. Someone not used to the life. Who didn't understand its strictures.

Because it was too easy for them to walk and too hard for her to leave.

Tapping the thumbs-up emoji—about as impersonal as an emoji got—she put down her phone and rejoined the baby name conversation as if a little piece of her heart hadn't just sheared right off.

It was a cold, grey morning the next day, which was a perfect match for Xiomara's gloomy mood as she walked into Edmund's rooms to be with Tavi and Phoebe for the ultrasound. She'd taken the coward's way out, arriving a few minutes after the royal couple had entered and with Xavier by her side. There'd been no need for him to accompany her into the room and he had looked momentarily puzzled when she'd asked but he had, of course, obliged.

She didn't feel great about using Xavier as a barrier between herself and Edmund but nothing demonstrated the disparity in their lives like arriving with personal security in tow. And thank God she had, because just the sight of Edmund was like a brick to her heart, a rush of feelings almost felling her at the knees.

How could she feel so…*much* after such a short acquaintance?

He was still dressed casually, in a navy pair of chinos and a grey polo shirt, but he'd shaved, she noted absently, the scruff he'd been sporting since she'd met him nowhere to be seen. She liked the scruff. She liked the scruff *a lot*.

She liked that he knew exactly how to use it to its most lethal effect.

But she liked the cleanshaven version of him

too. He looked more formal, more businesslike, more *renowned foetal medicine specialist*. This was the guy she'd first seen on the internet. Not the guy from the Seychelles. Or the apartment in Kensington. Or the cottage in Cornwall.

This guy was one hundred percent Harley Street, and God knew she needed that right now.

'Good morning, Xio,' he murmured from his position at the ultrasound machine.

In her peripheral vison she saw Phoebe and Tavi exchange *a look*. The kind of look married couples exchanged in that weird ESP thing that seemed to go hand in hand with a gold band.

Xio. Why…why? If he'd called her Xiomara she'd have been on the front foot. But *Xio* put her right back in the cottage, in front of that window, her breasts bared to the world, her head tossed back, as he came inside her.

And she suspected he knew that.

'Good morning.' Xiomara put every ounce of demure princess she had into her reply as she left Xavier's side. She'd pulled her hair back into a severe ponytail and she was conscious of it brushing between her shoulder blades as she crossed to Phoebe, who was already on the bed, her shirt rucked up, a sheet covering to just under her bump.

She slid in beside Tavi, which put her directly opposite Edmund.

'How was your dinner last night?' Edmund asked Phoebe conversationally as he squirted warm goop on her belly with one hand whilst twisting a couple of knobs on the console with the other.

'Well, I had a hankering for a Super Club from Pret so we got a delivery.'

Xiomara briefly shut her eyes at being caught in a lie. When she opened them again it was to find Edmund watching her, one eyebrow slightly raised.

'Octavio got a Chicken Caesar and bacon,' Phoebe continued, oblivious, 'which I quite fancied when it arrived so I ate half of that.' She shot her husband an apologetic look. 'And Xiomara got her usual posh Cheddar and pickle, but she only ate half of hers and handed it over to Octavio to finish, but I intercepted it and ate that as well because I'm suddenly ravenous all the time.'

His gaze lingered on her for a beat longer before Edmund turned his attention to Phoebe and he said congenially, 'My favourite is their egg and mayo.'

Xiomara could have kissed him for that. Not for not calling her out but for running with Phoebe's detailed conversation about what they'd all eaten last night, which he surely didn't care about but he didn't try to interrupt either. It was as if he knew, as Xiomara did, that Phoebe was apprehensive about the ultrasound and was letting her chatter calm her nerves.

'Ooh, yes, that one's good too. Also, their Hoisin duck wrap is chef's kiss.' She gave an apologetic little half laugh. 'Sorry, I'm rambling. But we

192   FORBIDDEN FLING WITH THE PRINCESS

don't have Pret in Castilona *or* New Zealand and they make really good sandwiches.'

'They do,' he agreed with a warm, reassuring smile. 'Now, shall we do this?'

'Oh, yes—' she breathed a relieved sigh '—please.'

Flicking the nearby wall switch, he killed the overhead lights and, with one swipe of the transducer, the twins were, once again, on the screen. Phoebe made a throaty noise and grabbed Xiomara's hand as Tavi pressed a kiss to her forehead.

'There they are,' Edmund announced. 'Oh, yes, that looks much better.'

'Really?' Phoebe asked, her voice suspiciously husky.

Edmund grinned. 'Really.' He angled the transducer as he fiddled with the console. 'The amniotic sac of the donor twin is significantly bigger and he has a full bladder.'

The ultrasound continued, with Xiomara sure that Edmund was spending much longer for the sake of allaying parental anxiety than he might normally and, again, she could have kissed him. He answered all their questions and took his time examining everything, reiterating several times how happy he was with the results.

By the time he'd wiped off Phoebe's belly, she and Tavi were a very happy King and Queen.

'Now, let me stress,' he said as Phoebe pulled her shirt down, 'TTTS usually takes a couple of weeks to fully resolve, so I want you to have another ultrasound next week in Castilona. I will be in touch with Dr García and will make sure she gets all my notes and copies of the scans.'

'Thank you,' Octavio said, holding out his hand. 'I don't know what we would have done without you.'

Tavi's statement took Xiomara right back to the beach the day their identity had been blown. Was it only two days ago? That was what Raymond had said about Edmund, too. Except he'd said *your man.* Those two words had caused a tiny little flutter at the time but now they made her heart ache.

Edmund waved the compliment aside as he continued. 'I'm going to be in Africa for four weeks from Monday. I'll be fairly remote and mostly uncontactable.'

Xiomara had known he was going to Africa and the fact he would be out of range should be welcome news because that meant it would be a clean break. Not that they'd been *together* to break up, but it would be cold turkey. No one a.m. *miss-you* phone calls or long texting sessions.

Despite the knowledge, her heart ached a little more.

'Too remote for Xiomara to land in a helicopter?' Octavio asked, a smile on his face.

She tensed as Edmund flicked a gaze his way. 'Even for her, yes,' he said with a slight smile before returning his attention to Octavio. 'But I'll make sure that Dr García has contact details for a

194   FORBIDDEN FLING WITH THE PRINCESS

colleague of mine—Kimberly Kwan. In case anything crops up—' he put up his hand as Phoebe opened her mouth and smiled gently '—not that I think it will.' Phoebe shut her mouth and smiled ruefully. 'Just for some peace of mind, that's all,' he assured her. 'Or even if you want to discuss anything or have *any* kind of worries or concerns, Kimberly is excellent.'

'Thank you,' Octavio said. 'That's most appreciated and I know Lola will also value the backup.'

'When are you flying back to Castilona?' he asked as he absently wiped the transducer with an anti-bacterial wipe.

'The plane is leaving in a few hours,' Phoebe confirmed.

It was probably only Xiomara who noticed the way Edmund's hand faltered a little as he wiped. But it would be stupid to read too much into it.

'I was just wondering how much activity Phoebe should do between now and the end of the pregnancy?' Octavio enquired. 'Our calendar is always full but with the revelries for the annual festival starting next week, it's more so than usual. A lot of different events, early starts, late nights.'

'I would advise trying to take it as easy as possible,' Edmund said as he slotted the transducer back in its holder. 'Twin births always carry a higher risk of early labour and the TTTS adds an extra layer to that risk. Are you able to take a step back, just as a precaution?'

Phoebe nodded as she rubbed a hand absently over her belly. 'I can work with my team to see what can be moved around and modified.'

'Nonsense.' Octavio shook his head. 'Of course you must step back.' He tipped his chin at his cousin. 'Xiomara can take over your commitments.'

'Tavi.' Phoebe gave a half laugh as she shook her head at her husband. 'Xiomara is already busy enough as patron of the festival and maybe—' she bugged her eyes at her husband '—she has other things she'd rather be doing.'

Xiomara's cheeks grew warm at the implication and she daren't look at Edmund. 'Of course I can do that,' she jumped in to assure Tavi. There was no hesitation on her part. It was a no-brainer. It was what Xiomara did as part of her service to the family and her country—made things as easy as possible. It was what she'd *always* done. Even now, she was shifting dates around in her head.

The fact that Edmund's eyes were hot on her profile only made her more determined. The extra workload would keep her so busy she wouldn't have time to miss him, that was something.

'Xiomara—' Phoebe shook her head as she briefly side-eyed Edmund '—no.'

'It's fine,' Xiomara assured her breezily as she squeezed Phoebe's hand and tried to convey with her eyes that everything was okay. That *she* was

196 FORBIDDEN FLING WITH THE PRINCESS

okay. That she and Edmund had been a dalliance but it was over now and she was *fine*.

That her first priority was always Castilona.

'Good.' Octavio nodded. 'That's settled.'

Phoebe sighed as she looked between the cousins then rolled her eyes as she glanced at Edmund, which caused his lips to quirk. 'Take the offer,' he said. 'Trust me, twin pregnancy can be extra tiring. By the time your little ones are born, you'll be pleased you did.'

Once again, Xiomara found herself wanting to kiss him. She knew Phoebe still struggled with the demands royalty made on their lives and found it slightly bewildering. Also, weird. She didn't understand how hereditary service was ingrained in the fabric of their lives. How could she? No one could, unless it was imprinted into their DNA.

'Seeing as how everyone has ganged up on me, I guess I'll have to,' she said. But she was more bemused than annoyed.

Octavio kissed her forehead. 'Don't worry, there'll be plenty more years for Castilona to see their Queen.'

A kick somewhere in the vicinity of Xiomara's heart had her looking away from the frank display of love and devotion, which was a mistake as her eyes landed squarely on Edmund, who had also averted his gaze—to Xiomara. Suddenly, they were looking at each other and she felt as if every moment they'd shared these past few days

AMY ANDREWS 197

was replaying on an invisible strip of celluloid between them.

Every touch, every kiss, every intimate moment.

But also, the walks along the beach and the even longer conversations as they lazed in bed, all loose and warm in a tangle of limbs. The picnic and cooking together. Trinket shopping in St Ives.

His gaze dropped to where the sea glass pendant hovered at the rise of her cleavage and the air in her lungs turned to molten heat, each breath viscous as honey.

'C'mon, *querida*,' Octavio said, 'let's get back to the consulate and get ready to fly out.'

Edmund dragged his attention back to the royal couple. 'It will be nice to get back home.'

Octavio smiled. 'You have no idea. Your city is grand and exciting but I miss the slower pace of life and the predictable mellow sunshine of our summer.'

'Yes—' Edmund grimaced '—our summers can be a bit of a mixed bag.'

He helped Phoebe down from the bed and Xiomara was grateful for the distraction as a flurry of thank-yous and goodbyes ensued. She accompanied them to the door, Xavier close on her heels.

'Can you give me a moment?' she said to Tavi as he passed her by. 'I'll be down shortly.'

He glanced over his shoulder into the office. 'Everything okay?' he asked her in Spanish.

No. Everything was not okay. But it would be.

198   FORBIDDEN FLING WITH THE PRINCESS

She nodded and replied, 'Of course, won't be long,' also in Spanish.

Xavier raised an eyebrow. 'Do you want me to stay?' He also spoke in Spanish, his voice a low murmur.

'No.' She shook her head. 'Thank you.'

He lingered for a moment and she gave a little nod for extra reassurance, teaming it with a small grateful smile for the man who she'd probably spent more time with than any other in recent years. With one last glance at Edmund, Xavier slipped out of the door and it clicked shut.

Long drawn-out moments of silence followed the click as Xiomara's eyes drifted to Edmund, who was now sitting on the edge of his desk, his leg swinging a little. Staying near the door, her gaze ate him up, roving over the casual fall of his hair to the rangy brawn of his frame to the perfect delineation of his leg muscles in those chinos.

Despite their short acquaintance, she'd come to know every inch of him so intimately and the thought of never seeing him again sat like a lump of cold porridge in her stomach.

'So—' he cocked an eyebrow '—this is the final goodbye, huh?'

Part of Xiomara had expected him to challenge her over her little white lie from last night. Many other men would have but she should have known he wasn't one of them. He wasn't some petulant, feckless rich-boy who was too used to, and overly

AMY ANDREWS 199

fond of, attention. He wasn't about to pout and make a scene. He was a grown man with his own life to lead.

He'd clearly understood why she'd avoided going to his place, or at least that she had her reasons that were none of his business. Because they weren't in any kind of relationship, which meant she wasn't accountable to him. And he wasn't accountable to her.

'Yes.' Xiomara swallowed against the lump in her throat.

Final. It sounded so, well…final.

But this being anything other than a two-week fling would be absurd. Even thinking it *could* be more was absurd. She wasn't some giddy, flighty *girl* who thought every man who kissed her was *the one.* She'd known what this was going in and nothing had changed. It had been spontaneous and thrilling and opportunistic but it had been a *liaison* and nothing more.

Yes, it had been like nothing else she had ever experienced and just looking at him flushed her body with a kind of yearning that was more than physical, but wishing and hoping and dreaming was for other women. Not for princesses with obligations and commitments and subjects who expected her focus to be on them and their beloved Castilona.

Still, she was pleased she'd dressed for the occasion in a silky bronze pants suit that clung and moulded to her hips and breasts, the cleavage daring, the solid weight of the sea glass pendant drawing the eye. She'd made an impression the day she'd walked into his life; it was only fitting that she left him with an equally flashy impression the day she walked out of it.

'That is a very great shame,' he murmured.

It was, it really was. She just hadn't expected him to feel the same way, let alone say it out loud. Her stomach lurched at his admission and she tensed her legs and straightened her spine lest she somehow betrayed her inner uproar.

She forced herself to shrug casually instead. 'This was never anything more than an affair of convenience.'

But even as she said the words, Xiomara knew they were wrong. So wrong they clawed at her throat. It was never *meant* to be anything but, right from the start, their chemistry had been more than sexual.

There'd been synergy as well.

'We both knew that,' she added for good measure because he couldn't know that she was feeling more things than she should after such short acquaintance.

She might be royal and trained to display poise and dignity at all times but she suddenly felt terribly gauche in front of this very accomplished man and couldn't bear the thought that he might

AMY ANDREWS   201

think her asinine or silly for allowing herself to *catch feelings.*

He regarded her for long moments, his leg gently swinging, but didn't say anything. Xiomara wished she could tell what he was thinking like she'd been able to in Cornwall, when there'd been an openness between them she'd relished. But there was a reserve there now and she just didn't know.

'It seems like you're going to be busy.'

Xiomara nodded. And so was he. It was the perfect way for them both to move forward and not look back. 'August is always busy. Planning for the festival will be in full swing upon our return and as the patron that takes up much of my time.'

'And now you have Phoebe's engagements too.'

'Yes.' Xiomara nodded. 'There'll be plenty to do.'

He folded his arms. 'And is that what you want?'

She frowned. 'To be busy?' Hell, yes, it was exactly what she wanted.

'To be at the King's beck and call?'

Xiomara blinked. He'd challenged her similarly on the first day they'd met and here he was almost two weeks later, challenging her again. *Only he knew her better now.* He knew how intrinsically she was entwined with Castilona. How it wasn't just the place of her birth and where she lived but how she'd been raised to *serve* it as a member of the house of de la Rosa.

She was Castilona. Castilona was her.

202 FORBIDDEN FLING WITH THE PRINCESS

And it wasn't fair of him to reduce her life to one of brainless royal subservience. It might look like that to him, but *the King* was her cousin and newly ascended to the throne. If she could ease his burden while his focus was split between the demands of his people and the anxiety over his wife and unborn babies, then that was what she'd do.

Because that was what *family* did.

A spike of irritation needled at her brain and she could feel herself morphing into the haughty princess from that beach on the Seychelles, gathering her carefully chosen clothes and famous royal composure like armour around her. 'Castilona is my country. Everything I do is for my *country*.'

He nodded. 'It just…seems to me that the diplomacy required in what you do has given you this extraordinary skill set as well as incredible connections that could be useful in many fields of employment.'

Xiomara raised an eyebrow to cover her confusion. 'I have a job.' Sure, it wasn't exactly defined and she often felt like a jack-of-all-trades-master-of-none, but variety wasn't a bad thing. And she *was* going to speak to Tavi about clarifying her position—after the babies arrived.

'Princess?'

She stiffened. There was no contempt in his voice. It was very matter-of-fact. But Xiomara couldn't help but feel judged by him, just as she had that first day. 'Yes?'

AMY ANDREWS   203

'What if I was to offer you a job? With the Institute.'

Xiomara blinked. Okay...*that* she hadn't expected. But her pulse did a crazy little tap dance anyway as her brain grappled with what the offer meant. Had he put it out there because he wanted to see her again? It was a tantalizing thought—too tantalizing—and she quashed it before it could take root. Sure, plenty of minor European royals held down jobs, but they didn't have a full schedule of royal commitments as well.

So, how would that even work?

'I don't understand...' Xiomara shook her head as she leaned against the shut door, its solid presence at her back exactly what she needed after the startling suggestion. 'What kind of job?'

'Well...' his lips curved into a warm smile '—the Institute has just come into possession of one million pounds. You could help us spend it.'

Xiomara returned the smile despite the riotous state of her feelings. There was something about the laidback way Edmund didn't take himself too seriously that had her body lighting up from the inside and she was glad once again for the solid support of the door. She'd seen him at his serious professional best and yet he had a knack for knowing when to let that all go.

Yes, he was driven and committed but it wasn't his *whole* being.

Unlike herself, who found it impossible to separate out the princess from the woman. They were one and the same. Except maybe when she'd been wrapped up naked in Edmund's arms.

Everything in her life, it seemed, was serious, every element weighed down by such enormous responsibility and...*gravity*. Maybe that was why Edmund's suggestion felt so damn seductive.

Or maybe it was just the thought of being around him.

'The charity side of the Institute is always looking for ways to raise funds. There's a large committee that coordinates all these activities and there are any number of events that you could be involved with from an organizational standpoint or in an ambassadorial role. Certainly, your presence at functions would add a level of gravitas that tends to loosen the grip on wallets.'

Oh...

Time stood still for a moment as a hot spike of disappointment lanced straight through Xiomara's middle. So, he wanted her *gravitas*. Not her. Not what they'd shared.

He wanted her *royalness*.

Foolishly, she had thought Edmund was the only person who'd ever seen the woman first, not the princess. Who hadn't given a hoot for her pedigree.

Apparently not...

CHAPTER ELEVEN

XIOMARA GOT IT, of course. It made sense.

A real-life princess associated with your charity was quite the coup and would indeed lead to increased donations. But that didn't stop the tsunami of dismay body-slamming her from every direction, her heart thudding loud and slow like a warning gong.

'So, you think I should...' Xiomara was careful to keep her voice light and not betray how much his suggestion had hurt '...be at *your* beck and call instead?'

Her raised eyebrow and calm smile would have won her an Oscar had she been an actress in a movie. It certainly felt like she was playing a part now, existing somewhere outside her body as she mentally shored up her disintegrating poise.

'No... Xio.' He stood, pushing away from the desk. 'I'm sorry, I didn't mean...'

He prowled towards her and if Xiomara could have backed up more she would have. As if sensing the tension in her body, Edmund slowed and stopped when he got within touching distance. 'That came out all wrong.'

He shoved a hand through his hair, which bulged

206   FORBIDDEN FLING WITH THE PRINCESS

his pecs and biceps, and Xiomara wanted nothing more than to rewind a day so she could just slide her arms around his waist and lay her cheek on his chest. But perhaps this was for the best. This awkwardness.

'Apologies. What I should have said is that you're young and accomplished and articulate. You're more experienced in many ways than most people your age and you're not intimidated by anything or anyone. Which is a rare thing. And you don't take no for an answer.' His lips lifted in the ghost of a smile. 'You'd be an amazing asset to *any* organisation or workplace.'

His gaze captured hers, blazing with sincerity, his words mollifying her a little. But they didn't change the facts of her life. Smiling graciously to acknowledge his clarification, she said, 'Thank you, but I'm happy with what I do.'

She *was* happy, damn it. And after the twins arrived she'd look at carving out a role for herself that didn't just involve smiling, waving and making small talk, that was more than ornamental.

'Okay.' He nodded. 'Just…food for thought.'

Xiomara had no doubt she'd probably think of little else. That this conversation would become like a burr in her shoe, niggling and prickling. Still, that was far preferable to thinking about him hot and hard and naked, the span of his chest and the swell of his shoulders rising over her as he drove her to climax night after night.

'Well...' Xiomara shook the images from her head as she straightened, the support of the door gone now, the action edging her a little closer to Edmund, charging the air with a very familiar frisson '... I really shouldn't keep Xavier waiting any longer.'

Another nod from Edmund as his gaze sought and locked on hers, the charge intensifying as they stared at each other, all that had been between them pulsing bright and reckless in a moment heady with anticipation. He leaned in then and Xiomara's breathing stuttered for a beat.

Oh, no...he was going to kiss her.

Step back. She needed to step back. But Xiomara didn't know how to resist this pull he exerted. He inched closer and she was in his thrall, her breath strangling in her throat. But then he stopped, imperceptibly at first, then obviously as he reached for her hand.

For one crazy moment, Xiomara thought he was going to shake it. *Pleased to meet you. Have a nice day.* Which would have crushed her. But he didn't. Instead, he turned her hand over, lifted it to his mouth and, with his eyes fixed on hers, pressed his lips to it.

He kissed her hand like countless men—dignitaries, heads of state and Castilonian subjects—had done before. But nothing like that at the same time. There was nothing formal about the action. He kissed her hand like a man who had kissed her in many other, much more intimate places and they both knew it.

Smiling as he straightened, he murmured, 'I'll never forget you, Xiomara de la Rosa.'

Swallowing the rapid thickening in her throat, Xiomara smiled like she'd been taught to since she was old enough to understand it was required of her. 'Nor I you.'

Her tone was wistful as she pulled her hand from his. It was the last thing she *wanted* to do but it was the *sensible* thing. Ignoring her heavy heart, she opened the door and stepped outside, shutting it behind her with a final resounding click.

Shutting him out, literally and figuratively.

'Are you okay?' Xavier asked gently as he inspected her face.

She smiled and nodded even though the effort not to cry *burned* her eyes. How could she be okay when her stupid, feckless heart was breaking? It had been less than two weeks.

How was that even possible?

Xiomara sat at the table, staring absently out of the plane window as Tavi and Phoebe sat opposite and continued their baby name discussion. She was barely listening as the crystal-clear waters fringing Castilona came into view. The sight of her home from the air had always called to her. The tranquil lap of sea on sand filled her with peace and joy and contentment. The island had been her anchor, grounding her in history and tradition and family.

But today it felt more like a chain.

Especially with that hand kiss playing over and over in her mind. It was as chaste as any first kiss and yet she was obsessing over it just as much. In their brief acquaintance, Edmund had kissed her so much more intimately and yet there was something so…reverential about that kiss that clogged her throat with emotion and pricked at the backs of her eyes.

Had he felt the same level of emotion that she had over their parting? Confusion, reluctance, yearning. The look in his eyes as his mouth had brushed her skin had seemed to be saying *Don't go,* but she didn't trust her ability to interpret anything when it came to the enigmatic doctor she'd known for such a short time.

She was far too enamoured to trust her instincts where he was concerned.

And what if she'd been free to stay in London? Would he have wanted that? If she was a normal everyday woman, would he have just *asked* her to stay?

Or asked to see her again, at the very least?

The captain came over the intercom announcing their descent, bringing Xiomara out of the quagmire of her thoughts to once again focus on Tavi and Phoebe's conversation. She'd lost track of the number of boys' names that had been bandied around, from the traditional to those that would pay homage to Phoebe's New Zealand roots. There was also debate about the difference between the first-born twin's name and the second because the first would be King one day and the name should be given extra special consideration.

Which Xiomara understood on one hand, but made her want to shred her skin on the other.

Her father had been Tavi's father's twin. The second-born. A cosmic roll of the dice that had embittered her father and driven a wedge between the brothers. And it *had* been her father that was responsible for the ill will. Her Uncle Miguel—*King Miguel*—had been gracious and understanding and had tried to breach the gap on so many occasions. She remembered how often he had reached out the hand of peace during her childhood, only to have it rebuffed.

It had been *her* father who hadn't been able to handle the trick of fate that had been no more Miguel's fault than it had been his. But he'd taken it very personally and not only let it define him but let it fester. Even let it shape his decade-old reign as Regent while waiting for Tavi to come of age.

Castilona had become more isolated under her father's regency. More inward-looking. Less prosperous. It had taken a back seat on the global stage as it had become more protectionist. And that had had ramifications. International relations had suffered. Business and trade had suffered. Their wine exports had taken a massive hit.

But that had all, thankfully, changed with Octavio's ascension. Within the first month he had reestablished old trading links and ushered in a new age for Castilona. And the world had embraced them with open arms. So, the last thing Xiomara wanted to see was history repeating itself with these two precious baby boys.

Brothers should be close. They should be loving and supportive. They should build each other up. Not have one working behind the scenes to tear the other down. Not that Xiomara thought Phoebe and Tavi would allow such a rift to develop or that the degree of regalness of a name alone could cause a rift. But the twins would not grow up in a vacuum.

Tavi was now running through all the King's names for the past several hundred years and giving Phoebe a potted history of their reigns, looking for inspiration from the past. Phoebe had studied the history of Castilonian monarchy after her and Tavi's hasty nuptials but there was only so much a person could learn from books.

'Who cares about historical precedent?'

The impatient words were out before Xiomara could call them back, spilling into the space between them, abruptly ending the conversation. Phoebe's kind eyes blinked owlishly as Tavi's eyebrows raised.

'I think the people of Castilona might.'

212   FORBIDDEN FLING WITH THE PRINCESS

It was on the tip of Xiomara's tongue to say, *So what?* Too much of Tavi's life—*her* life—was dictated by Castilonian expectations. The monarchy—even under the more austere regency of her father—was beloved amongst the people and Tavi and Phoebe's wedding and the impending birth of their babies had added a much-needed sprinkle of fairy dust to the institution of the monarchy.

The Castilonian people adored their new King and Queen, so surely none would begrudge the young royal couple the experience of naming their own children without regard to centuries of tradition.

'Call them what you want, what any other parents would call their kids. Call them Beavis and Butt-Head if you like.'

Phoebe laughed, clearly tickled by the idea of a King Butt-Head. Tavi, on the other hand, was more serious. 'But we're not just any other parents.'

And that was it, right there. Like herself, Tavi could never disassociate himself from his role. He could never truly just be Octavio. Every hair on his head, every cell in his body, belonged to Castilona. And every action he took was predicated on how it would affect his people.

'Just…' Xiomara let out a heavy sigh '…choose something you like. Don't let this decision be dictated by royal protocols and what their futures might be.'

Xiomara knew that was a big ask as silence settled over the table. Husband and wife exchanged a puzzled look.

'Xiomara?' Tavi's voice was gentle when he eventually spoke. 'What's going on?'

She wished she knew. She wished there wasn't this surge of discontent and resentment over the strictures of royal life, simmering like a witches' brew in her gut and almost overwhelming her with the desire to scream.

'I just would hate for them to feel any kind of *heir and the spare* divide.'

Phoebe's swiftly indrawn breath had Xiomara wondering if she'd gone too far. Luckily, gone were the days when speaking truth to power could put a person's head on the chopping block.

'We would never make them feel like that,' she said quietly.

'Of course, you won't.' Xiomara gentled her voice as she reached across and squeezed the other woman's hand. Phoebe was new to all this, it was easy for her to be idealistic, whereas Xio and Tavi had lived the reality. 'But society *will*.'

She glanced at her cousin. 'Had my father been born two minutes earlier, he would have been King—not just a temporary Regent—and the fact that he was born second had a huge ripple effect on everyone around him, including the country.'

Tavi nodded and Xiomara could see he was thinking about those years too. How the poison of that perceived slight had leached into every decision Mauricio had made as Regent, regardless of the ramifications. How he had spent so much of these last months untangling all her father's bitter knots.

'I'm aware. It's just…a lot easier in theory than in practice. Balancing the personal with the traditional.'

'Tradition.' Xiomara shook her head in disgust.

Her entire life had been dictated by tradition. When she'd been younger she'd taken comfort from it, knowing it provided some kind of road map to follow. It was only as she'd grown older that she could see it for the double-edged sword it was, and suddenly Xiomara was impatient for change.

She knew that Tavi's goal to modernise the monarchy had been derailed by much bigger matters of state, not to mention the royal wedding and the complications with the babies. But, if anything, the royal babies had only amplified the issue.

'What if the twins were a boy and a girl?'

Tavi's brow furrowed as if he wasn't sure where this was going. 'Okay?'

'And the girl was born first, making her the elder. But according to our succession laws she cannot rule because she's a girl and that privilege would go to her brother.'

As a female de la Rosa in a male primogeniture system, Xiomara was especially sensitive to the topic. Not because she wanted to be Queen, but because it rankled that she—or any female—was considered less *able* merely because of her gender. It rankled even more so today with Edmund's job offer replaying over and over in her brain.

'Do you not think she would be just as capable of ruling as her brother? Do you not think *I* would be just as capable of ruling as *you*?'

'Of course you would be.' He cocked an eyebrow. 'You...want it?'

Xiomara huffed out a breath. '*No*, Tavi, I don't want it.' It was the last thing she wanted. 'But I don't think I or any other female de la Rosa should be excluded from it either, just because of our gender. I don't think girls in our family should be made to feel inferior and that their only worth is in the male babies they can produce for the line.'

'Hear, hear,' Phoebe murmured.

Tavi glanced between the two women fixing him with their gazes and held up his hands. 'You get no argument from me.'

'Good.' Xiomara nodded. 'You want to modernise the monarchy? Then start there. Do something about our archaic male succession laws. The British Royal Family altered theirs over a decade ago. It's about time we brought ours in line for future generations of de la Rosas.'

'You're right. I'll get onto it first thing tomorrow.'

Xiomara smiled at her cousin but the victory felt hollow and did nothing to take the edge off her irritability. Two weeks out of her normal life

216   FORBIDDEN FLING WITH THE PRINCESS

and suddenly everything about her existence felt meaningless and it *gnawed* at her.

'Anything else I can do for you?' he queried, amusement lighting his handsome features. 'Would you like a national holiday named after you? The keys to the city?'

He was joking but Xiomara was in no mood for jokes. 'Yes. I want a job. A proper job.'

Xiomara hadn't planned on putting any of this on Tavi's plate right now. Changes to the succession and a job for her could have waited. The last couple of weeks had been stressful and she hadn't wanted to add to that. She'd been fine with waiting until after the babies arrived and all was well. But he'd opened the door and she was too vexed by the lack of direction in her life and her own inertia to stay quiet any longer.

'I don't want to cut ribbons any more or take a visiting dignitary's wife on a wine tour or read out some innocuous speech that someone in the royal protocol office has written. Not *all* the time anyway. I want something I can get my teeth into. A role I can call my own. And I want to write my own damn speeches.'

The plane touched down then, startling Xiomara a little. She'd been so caught up in the conversation and the squall of emotions inside her, she hadn't been paying attention to the plane's descent. It was impossible to speak then as the muffled roar of the reverse thrusters reverberated through the cabin and the plane rocked and vibrated as it rapidly slowed. But she was aware of both Phoebe and Tavi watching her carefully—one curious, one concerned.

Phoebe was the first to speak as the plane slowed to a taxi and they could hear each other again. 'You seem unhappy.'

What? No. She wasn't unhappy. How could she be? That would be ridiculous, given her life of enormous privilege. But she wasn't…satisfied either. She *had* been, but the last two weeks had changed everything.

'I'm not,' she assured them with a quick smile. 'It's just… I'm twenty-seven years old. I want to do more with my life. Something meaningful.'

Tavi met her gaze. Xiomara knew that he, more than anyone, understood what she meant. Everyone assumed that being born into royalty meant you had no other life ambition, but that simply wasn't true. And she wasn't going to let it dictate her life any more.

'Good idea.' Tavi smiled. 'Something else to talk about tomorrow?'

Xiomara nodded. She could wait a day.

CHAPTER TWELVE

THE PLAZA CENTRAL was awash with sunshine and alive with merriment on the last Sunday in August. Throngs of people wearing wreaths of vine leaves in their hair were out enjoying the culmination of the Fiesta del Vino de Verano. Bunting of mini Castilonian flags crisscrossed overhead and fluttered in the light breeze. Building edifices, shopfronts and cafés that faced the square were decorated in vine leaves dripping with grapes, as were lampposts, flagpoles and bollards. Statues and figurines in fountains were given the same treatment.

Laughter was everywhere as children ran in between groups of festivalgoers and both local and tourists alike took their turn at stomping grapes with their bare feet in the plethora of wooden half barrels that littered the cobblestoned square. Guitar music drifted from somewhere, adding to the general hubbub along with a mix of languages, Spanish and English predominantly, but also a smattering of other European languages, giving the event a truly international feel.

Ed hadn't planned on being here. In fact, only yesterday he had a flight booked from Dar es Salaam to London. And then he'd arrived at the airport and just…changed his mind. On a whim.

Sure, he'd told himself, he needed a break before he went back to work in a few days. His time in Africa had been its usual mixed bag of rewarding and gruelling and a few days chilling on a Mediterranean island was just what the doctor ordered. Especially considering his last island holiday had been cut short.

He also needed to deliver an apology to Xiomara. To *Xio*. For his gaffe the day they'd parted in London. What on earth had possessed him to offer her a *job,* he had no idea. All that had done was trivialise her time-consuming role in the royal court.

But, in truth, neither of those were the real reasons he'd not boarded that plane to London.

He'd come to Castilona because he couldn't *not*. Because he *had* to see her. Because he'd missed her and hadn't been able to stop thinking about her. He'd known her for less than two weeks and been apart from her for four and they had been *interminable*.

It was ridiculous. He'd been *engaged* to Kelly and had never felt this constant restless, *reckless* need to be with her. To see her. To just be in the same room as her. It had invaded every moment of his days in Africa, from teaching in sophisticated university auditoriums, to performing life-saving foetal surgery in rudimentary hospitals, to

220   FORBIDDEN FLING WITH THE PRINCESS

pitching in at maternal health clinics held under mahogany trees on the outskirts of villages or in white tents in refugee camps.

Xio had formed a relentless drumbeat in his head.

Xio. Xio. Xio.

Her smile, the way her hair bounced around her head when she laughed, her graciousness. The way she talked and dressed and moved. The way she was with people. Sure, she'd been cool and haughty with him originally, but he knew her well enough now to know that was her façade for when she felt out of her depth. The more she was unsure of herself, the more she disappeared behind her princess veneer.

She'd not been like that with the parents of the little girl who had fallen at her feet on the beach. Or the father of the boy who had nearly drowned. Or with Xavier. Who was essentially *staff* and yet she treated him with deference and respect.

And Ed couldn't wait to see her again. He just hoped she felt the same way.

He hadn't let Xiomara know he was on Castilona because he knew that, as festival patron, she'd be busy and he didn't want to interfere with her day. He'd call her this evening and let her know he was here. In the meantime, he was content to wander for a while, soaking up the sights and sounds. And, as he scooped another spoonful of delicious paella into his mouth, the tastes.

He'd purchased it from one of the many market stalls that was stationed along one of the access roads to the plaza. It was rich and spicy and he sighed contentedly at the burst of flavours on his palate.

But then he heard the laugh—*her laugh*—cutting through the murmur of the crowds and the food suddenly turned to ash in his mouth.

Xiomara.

It *was* her laugh. He knew the sound intimately. He knew every inflection of it. The snort laugh when she was watching something funny on the television, the tinkly laugh when something delighted her, the hysterical laugh when she was being tickled, the low, self-deprecating laugh when she was poking fun at herself.

This laughter was pure joy and he turned, homing in on it, spotting her standing in a barrel in the middle of the square, encircled by a crowd. She was in a stripy boho dress, her arms bare, the skirt tucked up at the sides to lift the hem to just below her knees. The amber sea glass pendant she'd bought in St Ives played peekaboo with her cleavage.

There was another woman with her, also laughing, as they held each other's shoulders for purchase and watched their feet as they crushed grapes, their knees rising up and down, their calves splashed with dark red juice.

On her head, sitting atop her curls, was a simple

222   FORBIDDEN FLING WITH THE PRINCESS

leaf wreath. It was far from the tiara she'd been wearing in the photograph he'd found online the day they'd first met and, standing in a barrel with the hem of her dress splattered in grape juice, she was far from the formality of *that* princess.

But the people milling around clearly didn't care. They were smiling—beaming, actually—and clapping as they called out, '*Viva!*' and took pictures on their phones, clearly enamoured with their Princess getting her feet dirty. There were some paparazzi too, snapping away, but not many, and none were yelling her name or bothering her, as he had witnessed in the UK. Certainly, Xiomara wasn't paying them any heed—nobody was.

Well, almost nobody. Xavier, who Ed had spotted off to one side, was keeping an eagle eye, but there was no tension in his body like Ed had witnessed in London.

Ditching his finished food in a nearby bin, Ed let his feet take him in her direction, aware of the sudden extra beat of his heart. He made his way slowly, hanging back a little to just watch her and the utter joy on her face. Xavier clocked him but, if he was surprised, didn't show it, just tipped his chin in acknowledgement before returning his gaze to his protectee.

The woman in the barrel took a selfie with Xiomara, who grinned at the camera before she was helped out and two little girls with wreaths in their hair, one slightly older than the other, were lifted in—by their parents, he presumed—to join the Princess. She smiled and chatted to them in Spanish and held out her hands for them to take, which they did, smiling up at her, as dazzled as the rest of the crowd by her exuberance.

Xiomara led the girls around in a circle, reciting some song he didn't know, the girls giggling in response as they stomped with extra enthusiasm. More pictures were taken, then the girls were lifted out and an elderly man, his trousers rolled up to his knees, was helped in. Xiomara leaned close to hear what he said, then she laughed, a big hearty sound as if the old man had told a risqué joke, and Ed swore he could see the old guy's eyes twinkling from here.

They stomped then, Xiomara's curls bouncing as she got into the action, and his breath caught. She was *radiant* in the sunshine and he was in love with her.

There it was. As plain and simple as that.

Part of him wanted to dispute it because how could he possibly know *that* after such a short acquaintance? But it was indisputable. Overwhelmingly *irrefutable*. It was there in every in/out chug of his breathing, every lub-dub of his heartbeat. Somewhere in those two weeks he'd fallen hook, line and sinker for the Princess.

No. Not somewhere. *Day one*. That moment she'd stepped from that helicopter and strode across the white sand of a Seychelles beach, looked at him imperiously and demanded he go with her. She'd *wowed* him that day for sure, but he recognized now it had been much deeper than that. In that one bold move she had totally snatched his heart.

He'd been a goner from *that* moment, he just hadn't realised it until *this* moment.

And for a few seconds of pure utter joy, love flooded his system like a thousand laser lights all humming on together, the possibilities of a life together stretching endlessly in front of him. Then he looked around at the adoring crowds and the indulgent smiles and the sheer buzz surrounding her and he realised he wasn't the only one who loved her.

*They l*oved her, these people. And *she* loved them. Princess Xiomara de la Rosa could never ever truly be only his.

The laser lights switched off abruptly, deflating his chest, the joy in his heart turning to an ache. The crowd noise around him seemed to amplify, making it impossible to think. The high of moments ago crashed to a brutal low, his gut churning, his temples throbbing.

It wasn't that Ed didn't want to share her. Seeing her like this with her people filled him with pleasure—he could watch this all day. But he knew already he loved her too much to ask her to leave. Or to split her life, her loyalties, in two.

If, indeed, she even felt the same way.

AMY ANDREWS 225

And even if she did, how could he ask that of her when she was *incandescent* with happiness right now? When every part of him could see that she *belonged* here in Castilona?

His heart heavy, Ed slowly backed away, tamping down on his instinct to rush in and blurt out his feelings, sweep her up and carry her off. Xiomara's royal status added a level of complication that, now reality had set in, he knew deserved deeper thought and consideration. He was a logical guy— his job demanded it of him—there was no reason why this issue couldn't have a logical solution, too. He just had to go away and come up with a plan before he came back for her.

Because he would be back. Once he'd figured it out.

Turning away, he shuffled through the crowd, head down, not really looking where he was going as he started to turn the problem over in his mind. Someone stepped in his path and he sidestepped to avoid a collision, only to find two big black boots blocking his path again.

Frowning, Ed glanced up to discover Xavier standing in his way. 'Oh…hey.'

'Hey.' Xiomara's bodyguard nodded. 'Where are you going?'

'I'm heading back to London.'

He cocked an eyebrow. 'Without saying hello to the Princess?'

Both the eyebrow and the tone of voice left Ed

226 FORBIDDEN FLING WITH THE PRINCESS

in no doubt that Xavier was judging him. But he could live with that.

'I shouldn't have come today. She's busy with the festival. I'll call her next week.'

Xavier regarded him for long moments, not saying anything but not moving either. 'So, you're just going to let all this—' he glanced around the plaza '—intimidate you?'

Ed supposed he should be annoyed that Xavier was overstepping but the bodyguard obviously felt it was his role to look out for Xiomara in more than just a physical safety sense.

'Not at all,' he denied. He *wasn't* intimidated, but it made rushing in more complicated. Ed's gaze returned to the centre of the square, where he could just see Xiomara through a throng of people, her curls bobbing as she stomped on grapes with yet another person. 'They love her very much,' he said, his eyes fixed on her.

'They do.'

'And she loves them.'

'She does. But that's not the kind of love that keeps a person warm at night.'

Ed dragged his eyes from Xiomara to her bodyguard. 'No.'

'She hasn't been the same since returning from London.'

The news lifted Ed's heart. Was Xavier trying to tell him that Xiomara reciprocated his feelings? The mere thought made him a little dizzy. But that

AMY ANDREWS 227

still didn't remove the hurdles he could see at every turn. He hesitated. 'It's…complicated.'

'It is.'

Xavier's simple acknowledgement of the situation was appreciated. 'I need some time to think how we might navigate a life together.'

'I understand.' He nodded. 'But maybe—' he glanced at Xiomara again '—two brains are better than one?'

Ed followed his gaze at the same time the crowd parted a little and a ray of sunshine flooded her in warmth, holding her in its glory. It was like a sign from on high and his heart just about exploded out of his chest. Xavier was right. Ed had come all this way; he couldn't leave here without talking to her. Without telling her he loved her and begging her to love him back.

He didn't want to.

He'd spent four weeks in Africa wanting this— to see her—and now he was here he wasn't going to let hurdles and complications get in his way of holding her again.

Ed glanced at Xavier and stuck out his hand. 'You're right,' he said as they shook. 'Two brains are better than one.'

Xiomara was fine, *perfectly* fine. She'd been busy this past month, too busy to think about Edmund. Which had been a good thing. She'd proved to herself that she didn't need him, that it had been a

228 FORBIDDEN FLING WITH THE PRINCESS

one-off. An infatuation caused by his utter competence and proximity. And today was the culmination of Castilona's month of celebration and she was happy, damn it.

She would *not* think of him.

There was sun on her face and grape juice between her toes and she was home on Castilona, surrounded by people who loved her. She didn't need anything else in life. But then she looked up from her feet and Edmund was striding towards her in quad-hugging shorts and a pec-emphasising T-shirt, looking even better than she remembered…and she knew. She *one hundred percent* knew.

This wasn't infatuation.

This was *love*.

'Edmund?' she said breathily as he halted in front of her, the curious looks of the crowd around her fading away as he stared at her so intently she thought she might faint from how hard and fast her heart was beating.

'*Xio*,' he muttered, his amber eyes darkening to tawny.

And then he was reaching for her and she was reaching for him and his mouth was on hers, kissing her deep and hard, filling up her senses with his taste and smell, uncaring of their audience. Heat and lust and love coalesced into a raging torrent, flowing through her veins, deluging her every

AMY ANDREWS 229

sense as she held on and leaned in and moaned and opened to the quest of his tongue.

She'd missed him so damn much.

Hooting and hollering finally penetrated and Xiomara remembered where they were. Breaking off, she looked around at the crowd, who were teasing her good-naturedly, and she didn't even care that there were several paparazzi here who were going to cash in on her today.

Xiomara didn't care if the kiss was splashed over the pages of every newspaper and magazine and social media site in the world.

She loved Dr Edmund Butler and she *wanted* the world to know.

Smiling goofily at him, her heart did a little giddy-up to see him returning her smile with one equally as goofy. But what she craved was a very different kind of look that was not for public consumption. Glancing to her right, she found Xavier. 'Do you think you could find us somewhere close by?' she asked him in English.

The palace was too far away and she hadn't come in a car today. She didn't need to say *somewhere private*. Xavier knew what was required.

He nodded briskly. 'Follow me.'

Xiomara apologised to the crowd as Edmund helped her out of the barrel. She promised to return shortly as she dried off her feet and shoved them into her strappy flats. No one seemed to mind her hasty departure from the scene as they beamed at her knowingly.

How could they *not* know after that very, *very* public display of affection?

She and Edmund followed Xavier, who was walking at a reasonable clip. People greeted her as they passed by. They smiled affectionately and regarded Edmund curiously but they must have looked like they were on a mission because no one tried to detain them.

Still, it probably took a minute before Xavier turned into a deserted side alley. *The longest damn minute of Xiomara's life.* Then, almost immediately he stopped and opened a blue door to the right, flanked either side by pots of red geraniums.

'No one's home here,' Xavier said as he stood aside for them to enter. 'I'll wait outside.'

Xiomara didn't question the location and only barely remembered to say thank you before dragging Edmund inside the cool, dark interior, pushing him against the closed door and kissing the hell out of him, revelling in his groan and the wild thrill of his hands locking on her ass and holding her firm against the hardness of his body.

They didn't talk—hell, they barely came up for air. After four weeks without him, Xiomara was *starving*, almost beside herself with the need to touch and taste and feel him. And if the way he dominated the kiss and the rough heave of his breathing was any indication, he was just as desperate.

How had she lived apart from this man for four weeks? How had she survived? She couldn't get enough. She couldn't stop.

She *never* wanted to stop.

Unfortunately, he had other ideas, eventually breaking away from the kiss, to her mewled protest. Xiomara went back in for seconds but he cupped her face and held her firm, their harsh, erratic breaths mingling as he stared into her face.

'More,' she muttered, her gaze roving over his lips, wet from her kisses.

He chuckled at her impatience but quickly sobered. 'Soon,' he whispered. 'I just want to look at you for a moment.' And he did, he looked at her like she was his *everything,* and Xiomara knew she never wanted to be apart from him again. 'I love you,' he murmured.

Xiomara's breath caught on a sob. He *loved* her. This wildly accomplished man who had saved the lives of two precious babies and performed the same such miracles every day *loved her.*

And she loved him back.

'I'm in love with you,' he repeated, a slow smile lifting the corners of his mouth. 'And I know it's only been such a short time and I don't know how we're going to make it work, with my job and you being *a princess* and all, but if you're in love with me too then I know we'll figure it out, because I

232 FORBIDDEN FLING WITH THE PRINCESS

don't want any version of my life that doesn't include you by my side.'

If hearts could truly sing, Xiomara's was playing a symphony. One of those achingly romantic ones that rose to a crescendo and brought tears to her eyes.

'I am.' She gazed at him through two shimmering puddles. 'Wildly, deeply, desperately in love with you.'

She grinned then and suddenly they were back to goofy smiling.

'Same,' he murmured. 'Wildly. Deeply. Desperately.'

'Are you sure?' she asked, taking a moment to put aside the thrill and goofiness of it all to be serious. 'I don't want you to feel caged again.'

'The thing about cages,' he said as his eyes romanced over her face, 'is that when you find someone you want to be with for ever it doesn't feel like a cage any more. It just feels like home.'

Oh. This man. He undid her.

But… Her brow crinkled. The realities of her life were very different to most. 'My life is not exactly normal, so you need to be really sure.'

'I'm sure.' His gaze was earnest as he brushed his thumb across her cheekbone. 'Hell, Xio, I'm *that* sure I want *babies* with you.'

Xiomara was momentarily nonplussed. Now *that* she hadn't expected. 'You do?' He'd been so genuinely conflicted in Cornwall.

'Yeah.' He nodded. 'I get it now. I get why people change their minds about having children when they find that one special person. I want to create something amazing from this love and I want to watch our babies grow inside you and I want to love them and raise them in our home together. Wherever that might be.'

He smiled at her then, slow and sincere, and she believed him.

'There's so much to figure out,' she whispered, her head light and spinning but her heart solid and true.

'There is,' he agreed. 'But we'll do it together, okay?'

Xiomara nodded. 'Okay.'

And that was all she needed in this moment as their lips met because together started now.

EPILOGUE

Three months later...

THE LUSTY CRIES of Rafael Miguel de la Rosa—the baby that would one day be King of Castilona—filled the operating theatre as Ed, scrubbed and gowned and assisted by Lola García in similar garb, eased the second royal baby boy out of his watery home.

'And here's number two,' Ed announced.

The baby blinked at the bright light, snuffling a little as Lola clamped and cut the cord, and Ed indicated for the drape to be lowered a little so his parents could see their son as he held him up. Phoebe, an oxygen mask on her face, smiled through tears as Octavio, whose eyes were suspiciously glassy, kissed her forehead.

'You did it, *querida,*' he murmured. 'They're here.'

'What name do we have for this little one?' Ed asked.

'Rodrigo,' Octavio said. 'Rodrigo Tomas de la Rosa.'

Ed smiled although he knew it couldn't be seen behind the mask. Xiomara had told him all about their beloved Uncle Rodrigo who had finally been able to return earlier this year to his island home after almost two decades of exile thanks to her father. Sadly, he'd returned only to die, but his name would now forever live on in Octavio's son.

'Congratulations, mum and dad,' Ed said as he passed the babe, who was also now bawling as loud as his brother, into the warmed sterile towel being held by a waiting nurse. 'You have two beautiful baby boys.'

Of course, they were red and wrinkled and covered in blood and vernix but their lungs were obviously healthy and the fact they'd made it to thirty-eight weeks and were both almost seven pounds after their TTTS complication had given them the very best start in life.

He'd been honoured a week ago when Phoebe had asked him if he had some time in his schedule to perform a C-section at the clinic. It was well below his paygrade but Ed never got tired of that moment he pulled a small wet body into the world and his connection to these two small wet bodies made this moment even more special.

He and Xiomara had flown out of London yesterday afternoon, slipping into Castilona without fanfare to spend the night at the palace. This morning he'd been scrubbing up beside Lola at the clinic by eight a.m. and now, not even twenty minutes later, he'd delivered two new lives into the world.

236   FORBIDDEN FLING WITH THE PRINCESS

'Okay,' he said. 'Let's finish up here so you can go spend some time with your babies.'

'Yes, please,' Phoebe said.

Indicating that the drape should be raised, Ed and Lola quickly delivered the placenta then closed. At nine a.m. Phoebe and Tavi and the babies were being rolled out of the door. Fifteen minutes after that, Ed emerged from the swing doors of the theatre to find Xiomara in the anteroom where she'd been waiting for news. She was talking to Xavier who, since Xiomara had moved to London, had become head of security at the Clínica San Carlos.

After much discussion between the royal protection detail and Octavio, Ed and Xiomara had taken up residence in the private royal apartment at the Castilonian consulate in Belgravia. It fulfilled her security needs and also gave her the perfect base for her new job, which entailed representing Castilona at various cultural forums throughout Europe.

The first few weeks after the news of their relationship broke had been a little ridiculous with the paparazzi but then some private royal drug-riddled rave in Slovenia had been busted by the police and the paps had quickly moved on.

She stood and smiled at him as he entered and Ed's heart did its usual thunk at the sight of her, still not quite able to believe how lucky he was that she'd chosen him to share her life. Between the two of them they travelled a fair bit for their jobs and Xiomara usually returned home to Castilona every few weeks to fulfil what she called her 'part-time princess role' but that only made their reunions more intense.

Every time he saw her, his feelings got bigger and bigger. He'd never thought that could be possible but he was living, breathing proof that love multiplied. And multiplied.

'Is everything okay?' she asked anxiously as she crossed to him.

'Everything is perfect.' He grinned. 'Mother, babies *and* daddy are all doing well.'

She threw her arms around his neck and kissed him. Kissed him in a thoroughly indecent manner that made him forget entirely they weren't alone. Although by the time they came up for air, the room was empty.

'*Dios,* you look sexy in a pair of scrubs,' she murmured.

Ed chuckled as his feelings grew bigger again. 'I love you, Princess Xiomara Maria Fernanda de la Rosa.'

'I love you too, Dr Edmund Butler.'

Then he kissed *her*. And his love multiplied and multiplied and multiplied.

* * * * *

Look out for the next story in the
Royally Tempted trilogy

One Night to Royal Baby
by JC Harroway

And if you enjoyed this story, check out these
other great reads from Amy Andrews

Harper and the Single Dad
Nurse's Outback Temptation
Tempted by Mr. Off-Limits
A Christmas Miracle

All available now!

Get up to 4 Free Books!

We'll send you 2 free books from each series you try PLUS a free Mystery Gift.

FREE Value Over **$25**

Both the **Harlequin Presents** and **Harlequin Medical Romance** series feature exciting stories of passion and drama.

YES! Please send me 2 FREE novels from Harlequin Presents or Harlequin Medical Romance and my FREE gift (gift is worth about $10 retail). After receiving them, if I don't wish to receive any more books, I can return the shipping statement marked "cancel." If I don't cancel, I will receive 6 brand-new larger-print novels every month and be billed just $7.19 each in the U.S., or $7.99 each in Canada, or 4 brand-new Harlequin Medical Romance Larger-Print books every month and be billed just $7.19 each in the U.S. or $7.99 each in Canada, a savings of 20% off the cover price. It's quite a bargain! Shipping and handling is just 50¢ per book in the U.S. and $1.25 per book in Canada.* I understand that accepting the 2 free books and gift places me under no obligation to buy anything. I can always return a shipment and cancel at any time. The free books and gift are mine to keep no matter what I decide.

Choose one:
- ☐ **Harlequin Presents Larger-Print** (176/376 BPA G36Y)
- ☐ **Harlequin Medical Romance** (171/371 BPA G36Y)
- ☐ **Or Try Both!** (176/376 & 171/371 BPA G36Z)

Name (please print)

Address   Apt. #

City   State/Province   Zip/Postal Code

Email: Please check this box ☐ if you would like to receive newsletters and promotional emails from Harlequin Enterprises ULC and its affiliates. You can unsubscribe anytime.

Mail to the Harlequin Reader Service:
IN U.S.A.: P.O. Box 1341, Buffalo, NY 14240-8531
IN CANADA: P.O. Box 603, Fort Erie, Ontario L2A 5X3

Want to explore our other series or interested in ebooks? Visit www.ReaderService.com or call 1-800-873-8635.

---

*Terms and prices subject to change without notice. Prices do not include sales taxes, which will be charged (if applicable) based on your state or country of residence. Canadian residents will be charged applicable taxes. Offer not valid in Quebec. This offer is limited to one order per household. Books received may not be as shown. Not valid for current subscribers to the Harlequin Presents or Harlequin Medical Romance series. All orders subject to approval. Credit or debit balances in a customer's account(s) may be offset by any other outstanding balance owed by or to the customer. Please allow 4 to 6 weeks for delivery. Offer available while quantities last.

Your Privacy—Your information is being collected by Harlequin Enterprises ULC, operating as Harlequin Reader Service. For a complete summary of the information we collect, how we use this information and to whom it is disclosed, please visit our privacy notice located at https://corporate.harlequin.com/privacy-notice. Notice to California Residents – Under California law, you have specific rights to control and access your data. For more information on these rights and how to exercise them, visit https://corporate.harlequin.com/california-privacy. For additional information for residents of other U.S. states that provide their residents with certain rights with respect to personal data, visit https://corporate.harlequin.com/other-state-residents-privacy-rights/.

HPHM25